Willa Cather

VINTAGE **CATHER**

Willa Cather was born on December 7, 1873, in Back Creek
Valley, Virginia. Her father was a sheep farmer. When she was
nine the family moved to Nebraska, eventually settling in the
frontier village of Red Cloud. As a child Cather read vora-
ciously, learning Greek and Latin from a neighbor, and displayed
an early interest in science. At the University of Nebraska she
immersed herself in literary studies and began writing stories
and essays; following her graduation in 1895 she worked for
some years as a journalist and schoolteacher, living part of the
time in Pittsburgh and Washington, D.C., and visiting Europe.

Cather's first book, a collection of poetry called *April Twilights,* was published in 1903, followed two years later by a
book of short stories, *The Troll Garden*. In 1906 she accepted
a job in New York as editor at one of the great American
national magazines, *McClure's,* where she stayed for six years,
often doing the bulk of the work of putting out the magazine
herself. In 1908 she met the novelist Sarah Orne Jewett,
whose writing influenced her greatly, and with whom she
shared a close friendship until Jewett's death sixteen months later.
From 1912 on, Cather devoted herself entirely to writing. For
most of her adult life she was based in New York City, but she
traveled frequently; she was particularly influenced by her visits to the Southwest from 1912 onward, and to Quebec City
beginning in 1928. Her friends included Dorothy Canfield,
Mabel Dodge Luhan, Mary Austin, Sigrid Undset, Stephen
Tennant, Yehudi Menuhin, and Edith Lewis.

While Cather's first novel, *Alexander's Bridge* (1912), was not particularly successful, in the next—*O Pioneers!* (1913)—she firmly established the sense of place and the meticulous descriptive style that would inform her best work. She later wrote of *O Pioneers!*, "Since I wrote this book for myself, I ignored all the situations and accents that were then generally thought to be necessary." Her reputation was further enhanced by *The Song of the Lark* (1915) and *My Ántonia* (1918), and for the war novel *One of Ours* (1922) she received the Pulitzer Prize. *A Lost Lady* (1923), *My Mortal Enemy* (1926), and *Lucy Gayheart* (1935) were further evocations of the Midwestern setting, but in other works she explored a variety of landscapes and eras: in *The Professor's House* (1925) the contemporary Southwest; in *Death Comes for the Archbishop* (1927) the Southwest in the period of the Spanish missions, treated in what she called "the style of the legends"; in *Shadows on the Rock* (1931), seventeenth-century Quebec; and in her final novel, *Sapphira and the Slave Girl* (1940), the nineteenth-century Virginia of her own ancestors.

Cather's later stories were collected in *Youth and the Bright Medusa* (1920) and *Obscure Destinies* (1930). Of her approach to fiction, she wrote, "Art, it seems to me, should simplify. That, indeed, is very nearly the whole of the higher artistic process. . . . Any first-rate novel or story must have in it the strength of a dozen fairly good stories that have been sacrificed to it. A good workman can't be a cheap workman; he can't be stingy about wasting material, and he cannot compromise." Cather is regarded as one of the most important American novelists and was the recipient of many literary prizes and honors. She died in New York on April 24, 1947.

BOOKS BY WILLA CATHER

April Twilights
The Troll Garden
Alexander's Bridge
O Pioneers!
The Song of the Lark
My Ántonia
Youth and the Bright Medusa
One of Ours
A Lost Lady
The Professor's House
My Mortal Enemy
Death Comes for the Archbishop
Obscure Destinies
Shadows on the Rock
Lucy Gayheart
Sapphira and the Slave Girl
Five Stories
The Old Beauty and Others
Uncle Valentine and Other Stories

VINTAGE CATHER

Willa Cather

VINTAGE BOOKS

A Division of Random House, Inc.

New York

The pieces in this collection were published as follows:

"Flavia and Her Artists," "Coming, Aphrodite!," "A Gold Slipper,"
and "A Wagner Matinée" from *Collected Stories,* copyright © 1905, 1920
by Willa Cather. Selection from *O Pioneers!,* copyright © 1913 by Willa Cather.
Selection from *My Ántonia,* copyright © 1918 by Willa Cather.
Selection from *One of Ours,* copyright © 1922 by Willa Cather. Chapter One
from *The Professor's House,* copyright © 1925 by Willa Cather. "December Night"
from *Death Comes for the Archbishop,* copyright © 1927
by Willa Cather.

Library of Congress Cataloging-in-Publication Data
Cather, Willa, 1873–1947.
[Selections. 2004]
Vintage Cather / Willa Cather.
p.   cm.—(Vintage readers)
"A Vintage original"—T.p. verso.
Contents: "Flavia and her artists" from Collected stories—Selection from
O pioneers!—Selection from My Ántonia—"Coming, Aphrodite!" from
Collected stories—"A gold slipper" from Collected stories—"A Wagner matinée"
from Collected stories—Selection from One of ours—Chapter one from The
professor's house—"December night" from Death comes for the archbishop.
ISBN 1-4000-7746-X (trade pbk.)
I. Title.   II. Series.
PS3505.A87A6 2004
813'.52—dc22   2004049327

Book design by JoAnne Metsch

www.vintagebooks.com

Printed in the United States of America
10   9   8   7   6   5   4   3   2   1

CONTENTS

VINTAGE **CATHER**

FLAVIA AND HER ARTISTS

As the train neared Tarrytown, Imogen Willard began to wonder why she had consented to be one of Flavia's house party at all. She had not felt enthusiastic about it since leaving the city, and was experiencing a prolonged ebb of purpose, a current of chilling indecision, under which she vainly sought for the motive which had induced her to accept Flavia's invitation.

Perhaps it was a vague curiosity to see Flavia's husband, who had been the magician of her childhood and the hero of innumerable Arabian fairy tales. Perhaps it was a desire to see M. Roux, whom Flavia had announced as the especial attraction of the occasion. Perhaps it was a wish to study that remarkable woman in her own setting.

Imogen admitted a mild curiosity concerning Flavia. She was in the habit of taking people rather seriously, but somehow found it impossible to take Flavia so, because of the very vehemence and insistence with which Flavia demanded it. Submerged in her studies, Imogen had, of late years, seen very little of Flavia; but Flavia, in her hurried visits to

New York, between her excursions from studio to studio—
her luncheons with this lady who had to play at a matinée,
and her dinners with that singer who had an evening
concert—had seen enough of her friend's handsome
daughter to conceive for her an inclination of such vio-
lence and assurance as only Flavia could afford. The fact
that Imogen had shown rather marked capacity in certain
esoteric lines of scholarship, and had decided to specialize
in a well-sounding branch of philology at the Ecole des
Chartes, had fairly placed her in that category of "interesting people" whom Flavia considered her natural affinities,
and lawful prey.

When Imogen stepped upon the station platform she
was immediately appropriated by her hostess, whose com-
manding figure and assurance of attire she had recognized
from a distance. She was hurried into a high tilbury and
Flavia, taking the driver's cushion beside her, gathered up
the reins with an experienced hand.

"My dear girl," she remarked, as she turned the horses
up the street, "I was afraid the train might be late. M. Roux
insisted upon coming up by boat and did not arrive until
after seven."

"To think of M. Roux's being in this part of the world
at all, and subject to the vicissitudes of river boats! Why in
the world did he come over?" queried Imogen with lively
interest. "He is the sort of man who must dissolve and
become a shadow outside of Paris."

"Oh, we have a houseful of the most interesting people,"
said Flavia, professionally. "We have actually managed to
get Ivan Schemetzkin. He was ill in California at the close
of his concert tour, you know, and he is recuperating with

us, after his wearing journey from the coast. Then there is Jules Martel, the painter; Signor Donati, the tenor; Professor Schotte, who has dug up Assyria, you know; Restzhoff, the Russian chemist; Alcée Buisson, the philologist; Frank Wellington, the novelist; and Will Maidenwood, the editor of *Woman*. Then there is my second cousin, Jemima Broadwood, who made such a hit in Pinero's comedy last winter, and Frau Lichtenfeld. *Have* you read her?"

Imogen confessed her utter ignorance of Frau Lichtenfeld, and Flavia went on.

"Well, she is a most remarkable person; one of those advanced German women, a militant iconoclast, and this drive will not be long enough to permit my telling you her history. Such a story! Her novels were the talk of all Germany when I was there last, and several of them have been suppressed—an honour in Germany, I understand. 'At Whose Door' has been translated. I am so unfortunate as not to read German."

"I'm all excitement at the prospect of meeting Miss Broadwood," said Imogen. "I've seen her in nearly everything she does. Her stage personality is delightful. She always reminds me of a nice, clean, pink-and-white boy who has just had his cold bath, and come down all aglow for a run before breakfast."

"Yes, but isn't it unfortunate that she will limit herself to those minor comedy parts that are so little appreciated in this country? One ought to be satisfied with nothing less than the best, ought one?" The peculiar, breathy tone in which Flavia always uttered that word "best," the most worn in her vocabulary, always jarred on Imogen and always made her obdurate.

"I don't at all agree with you," she said reservedly. "I thought every one admitted that the most remarkable thing about Miss Broadwood is her admirable sense of fitness, which is rare enough in her profession."

Flavia could not endure being contradicted; she always seemed to regard it in the light of a defeat, and usually coloured unbecomingly. Now she changed the subject.

"Look, my dear," she cried, "there is Frau Lichtenfeld now, coming to meet us. Doesn't she look as if she had just escaped out of Walhalla? She is actually over six feet."

Imogen saw a woman of immense stature, in a very short skirt and a broad, flapping sun hat, striding down the hillside at a long, swinging gait. The refugee from Walhalla approached, panting. Her heavy, Teutonic features were scarlet from the rigour of her exercise, and her hair, under her flapping sun hat, was tightly befrizzled about her brow. She fixed her sharp little eyes upon Imogen and extended both her hands.

"So this is the little friend?" she cried, in a rolling baritone.

Imogen was quite as tall as her hostess; but everything, she reflected, is comparative. After the introduction Flavia apologized.

"I wish I could ask you to drive up with us, Frau Lichtenfeld."

"Ah, no!" cried the giantess, drooping her head in humorous caricature of a time-honoured pose of the heroines of sentimental romances. "It has never been my fate to be fitted into corners. I have never known the sweet privileges of the tiny."

Laughing, Flavia started the ponies, and the colossal

woman, standing in the middle of the dusty road, took off her wide hat and waved them a farewell which, in scope of gesture, recalled the salute of a plumed cavalier.

When they arrived at the house, Imogen looked about her with keen curiosity, for this was veritably the work of Flavia's hands, the materialization of hopes long deferred. They passed directly into a large, square hall with a gallery on three sides, studio fashion. This opened at one end into a Dutch breakfast-room, beyond which was the large dining-room. At the other end of the hall was the music-room. There was a smoking-room, which one entered through the library behind the staircase. On the second floor there was the same general arrangement; a square hall, and, opening from it, the guest chambers, or, as Miss Broadwood termed them, the "cages."

When Imogen went to her room, the guests had begun to return from their various afternoon excursions. Boys were gliding through the halls with ice-water, covered trays, and flowers, colliding with maids and valets who carried shoes and other articles of wearing apparel. Yet, all this was done in response to inaudible bells, on felt soles, and in hushed voices, so that there was very little confusion about it.

Flavia had at last builded her house and hewn out her seven pillars; there could be no doubt, now, that the asylum for talent, the sanatorium of the arts, so long projected, was an accomplished fact. Her ambition had long ago outgrown the dimensions of her house on Prairie Avenue; besides, she had bitterly complained that in Chicago traditions were against her. Her project had been delayed by Arthur's doggedly standing out for the Michigan woods, but Flavia knew well enough that certain of the *aves rares*—

"the best"—could not be lured so far away from the seaport, so she declared herself for the historic Hudson and knew no retreat. The establishing of a New York office had at length overthrown Arthur's last valid objection to quitting the lake country for three months of the year; and Arthur could be wearied into anything, as those who knew him knew.

Flavia's house was the mirror of her exultation; it was a temple to the gods of Victory, a sort of triumphal arch. In her earlier days she had swallowed experiences that would have unmanned one of less torrential enthusiasm or blind pertinacity. But, of late years, her determination had told; she saw less and less of those mysterious persons with mysterious obstacles in their path and mysterious grievances against the world, who had once frequented her house on Prairie Avenue. In the stead of this multitude of the unarrived, she had now the few, the select, "the best." Of all that band of indigent retainers who had once fed at her board like the suitors in the halls of Penelope, only Alcée Buisson still retained his right of entrée. He alone had remembered that ambition hath a knapsack at his back, wherein he puts alms to oblivion, and he alone had been considerate enough to do what Flavia had expected of him, and give his name a current value in the world. Then, as Miss Broadwood put it, "he was her first real one,"—and Flavia, like Mahomet, could remember her first believer.

The "House of Song," as Miss Broadwood had called it, was the outcome of Flavia's more exalted strategies. A woman who made less a point of sympathizing with their delicate organisms might have sought to plunge these phosphorescent pieces into the tepid bath of domestic life;

but Flavia's discernment was deeper. This must be a refuge where the shrinking soul, the sensitive brain, should be unconstrained; where the caprice of fancy should outweigh the civil code, if necessary. She considered that this much Arthur owed her; for she, in her turn, had made concessions. Flavia, had, indeed, quite an equipment of epigrams to the effect that our century creates the iron genii which evolve its fairy tales: but the fact that her husband's name was annually painted upon some ten thousand threshing machines, in reality contributed very little to her happiness.

Arthur Hamilton was born, and had spent his boyhood in the West Indies, and physically he had never lost the brand of the tropics. His father, after inventing the machine which bore his name, had returned to the States to patent and manufacture it. After leaving college, Arthur had spent five years ranching in the West and travelling abroad. Upon his father's death he had returned to Chicago and, to the astonishment of all his friends, had taken up the business— without any demonstration of enthusiasm, but with quiet perseverance, marked ability, and amazing industry. Why or how a self-sufficient, rather ascetic man of thirty, indifferent in manner, wholly negative in all other personal relations, should have doggedly wooed and finally married Flavia Malcolm, was a problem that had vexed older heads than Imogen's.

While Imogen was dressing she heard a knock at her door, and a young woman entered whom she at once recognized as Jemima Broadwood—"Jimmy" Broadwood, she was called by people in her own profession. While there was something unmistakably professional in her frank *savoir-faire,* "Jimmy's" was one of those faces to which the rouge never seems to stick. Her eyes were keen and grey as a windy April sky, and so far from having been seared by calcium lights, you might have fancied they had never looked on anything less bucolic than growing fields and country fairs. She wore her thick, brown hair short and parted at the side; and, rather than hinting at freakishness, this seemed admirably in keeping with her fresh, boyish countenance. She extended to Imogen a large, well-shaped hand which it was a pleasure to clasp.

"Ah! you are Miss Willard, and I see I need not introduce myself. Flavia said you were kind enough to express a wish to meet me, and I preferred to meet you alone. Do you mind if I smoke?"

"Why, certainly not," said Imogen, somewhat disconcerted and looking hurriedly about for matches.

"There, be calm, I'm always prepared," said Miss Broadwood, checking Imogen's flurry with a soothing gesture, and producing an oddly-fashioned silver match-case from some mysterious recess in her dinner-gown. She sat down in a deep chair, crossed her patent-leather Oxfords, and lit her cigarette. "This match-box," she went on meditatively, "once belonged to a Prussian officer. He shot himself in his bath-tub, and I bought it at the sale of his effects."

Imogen had not yet found any suitable reply to make to this rather irrelevant confidence, when Miss Broadwood turned to her cordially: "I'm awfully glad you've come, Miss Willard, though I've not quite decided why you did it. I wanted very much to meet you. Flavia gave me your thesis to read."

"Why, how funny!" ejaculated Imogen.

"On the contrary," remarked Miss Broadwood. "I thought it decidedly lacked humour."

"I meant," stammered Imogen, beginning to feel very much like Alice in Wonderland, "I meant that I thought it rather strange Mrs. Hamilton should fancy you would be interested."

Miss Broadwood laughed heartily. "No, don't let my rudeness frighten you. Really, I found it very interesting, and no end impressive. You see, most people in my profession are good for absolutely nothing else, and, therefore, they have a deep and abiding conviction that in some other line they might have shone. Strange to say, scholarship is the object of our envious and particular admiration. Anything in type impresses us greatly; that's why so many of us marry authors or newspaper men and lead miserable lives." Miss Broadwood saw that she had rather disconcerted Imogen, and blithely tacked in another direction. "You see," she went on, tossing aside her half-consumed cigarette, "some years ago Flavia would not have deemed me worthy to open the pages of your thesis—nor to be one of her house party of the chosen, for that matter. I've Pinero to thank for both pleasures. It all depends on the class of business I'm playing whether I'm in favour or not. Flavia is my second cousin, you know, so I can say whatever disagreeable things I choose with perfect good grace. I'm quite desperate for some one to laugh with, so I'm going to fasten myself upon you—for, of course, one can't expect any of these gypsy-dago people to see anything funny. I don't intend you shall lose the humour of the situation. What do you think of Flavia's infirmary for the arts, anyway?"

"Well, it's rather too soon for me to have any opinion at all," said Imogen, as she again turned to her dressing. "So far, you are the only one of the artists I've met."

"One of them?" echoed Miss Broadwood. "One of the *artists?* My offence may be rank, my dear, but I really don't deserve that. Come, now, whatever badges of my tribe I may bear upon me, just let me divest you of any notion that I take myself seriously."

Imogen turned from the mirror in blank astonishment, and sat down on the arm of a chair, facing her visitor. "I can't fathom you at all, Miss Broadwood," she said frankly. "Why shouldn't you take yourself seriously? What's the use of beating about the bush? Surely you know that you are one of the few players on this side of the water who have at all the spirit of natural or ingenuous comedy?"

"Thank you, my dear. Now we are quite even about the thesis, aren't we? Oh! did you mean it? Well, you *are* a clever girl. But you see it doesn't do to permit oneself to look at it in that light. If we do, we always go to pieces, and waste our substance a-starring as the unhappy daughter of the Capulets. But there, I hear Flavia coming to take you down; and just remember I'm not one of them; the artists, I mean."

Flavia conducted Imogen and Miss Broadwood downstairs. As they reached the lower hall they heard voices from the music-room, and dim figures were lurking in the shadows under the gallery, but their hostess led straight to the smoking-room. The June evening was chilly, and a fire had been lighted in the fireplace. Through the deepening dusk the firelight flickered upon the pipes and curious weapons on the wall, and threw an orange glow over the Turkish hangings. One side of the smoking-room was entirely of glass, separating it from the conservatory, which was flooded with the white light from the electric bulbs. There was about the darkened room some suggestion of certain chambers in the Arabian Nights, opening on a court of palms. Perhaps it was partially this memory-evoking suggestion that caused Imogen to start so violently when she saw dimly, in a blur of shadow, the figure of a man, who sat smoking in a low, deep chair before the fire. He was long, and thin, and brown. His long, nerveless hands drooped from the arms of his chair. A brown moustache shaded his mouth, and his eyes were sleepy and apathetic. When Imogen entered, he rose indolently and gave her his hand, his manner barely courteous.

"I am glad you arrived promptly, Miss Willard," he said with an indifferent drawl. "Flavia was afraid you might be late. You had a pleasant ride up, I hope?"

"Oh, very, thank you, Mr. Hamilton," she replied, feeling that he did not particularly care whether she replied at all.

Flavia explained that she had not yet had time to dress for dinner, as she had been attending to Mr. Will Maiden-wood, who had become faint after hurting his finger in an obdurate window, and immediately excused herself. As she left, Hamilton turned to Miss Broadwood with a rather spiritless smile.

"Well, Jimmy," he remarked, "I brought up a piano box full of fireworks for the boys. How do you suppose we'll manage to keep them until the Fourth?"

"We can't, unless we steel ourselves to deny there are any on the premises," said Miss Broadwood, seating herself on a low stool by Hamilton's chair, and leaning back against the mantel. "Have you seen Helen, and has she told you the tragedy of the tooth?"

"She met me at the station, with her tooth wrapped up in tissue paper. I had tea with her an hour ago. Better sit down, Miss Willard." He rose and pushed a chair toward Imogen, who was standing peering into the conservatory. "We are scheduled to dine at seven, but they seldom get around before eight."

By this time Imogen had made out that here the plural pronoun, third person, always referred to the artists. As Hamilton's manner did not spur one to cordial intercourse, and his attention seemed directed to Miss Broadwood, in so far as it could be said to be directed to any one, she sat down facing the conservatory and watched him, unable to decide in how far he was identical with the man who had first met Flavia Malcolm in her mother's house, twelve years ago. Did he at all remember having known her as a little girl, and why did his indifference hurt her so, after all these years? Had some remnant of her childish affection for him gone on living, somewhere down in the sealed caves of her consciousness, and had she really expected to find it possible to be fond of him again? Suddenly she saw a light in the man's sleepy eyes, an unmistakable expression of interest and pleasure that fairly startled her. She turned quickly in the direction of his glance, and saw Flavia, just entering, dressed for dinner and lit by the effulgence of her most radiant manner. Most people considered Flavia handsome, and there was no gainsaying that she carried her five-and-thirty years splendidly. Her figure had never grown matronly, and her face was of the sort that does not show wear. Its blond tints were as fresh and enduring as enamel,—and quite as hard. Its usual expression was one of tense, often strained, animation, which compressed her lips nervously. A perfect scream of animation, Miss Broadwood had called it—created and maintained by sheer, indomitable force of will. Flavia's appearance on any scene whatever made a ripple, caused a certain agitation and recognition, and, among impressionable people, a certain uneasiness. For all her sparkling assurance of manner, Flavia was certainly always ill at ease, and even more certainly anxious. She seemed not convinced of the established order of material things, seemed always to conceal her feeling that the walls might crumble, chasms open, or the fabric of her life fly to the winds in irretrievable entanglement. At least this was the impression Imogen got from that note in Flavia which was so manifestly false.

Hamilton's keen, quick, satisfied glance at his wife had recalled to Imogen all her inventory of speculations about them. She looked at him with compassionate surprise. As a child she had never permitted herself to believe that Hamilton cared at all for the woman who had taken him away from her; and since she had begun to think about them again, it had never occurred to her that any one could become attached to Flavia in that deeply personal and exclusive sense. It seemed quite as irrational as trying to possess oneself of Broadway at noon.

When they went out to dinner, Imogen realized the completeness of Flavia's triumph. They were people of one name, mostly, like kings; people whose names stirred the imagination like a romance or a melody. With the notable exception of M. Roux, Imogen had seen most of them before, either in concert halls or lecture rooms; but they looked noticeably older and dimmer than she remembered them.

Opposite her sat Schemetzkin, the Russian pianist, a short, corpulent man, with an apoplectic face and purplish skin, his thick, iron-grey hair tossed back from his forehead. Next the German giantess sat the Italian tenor—the tiniest of men—pale, with soft, light hair, much in disorder, very red lips and fingers yellowed by cigarettes. Frau Lichtenfeld shone in a gown of emerald green, fitting so closely as to enhance her natural floridness. However, to do the good lady justice, let her attire be never so modest, it gave an effect of barbaric splendour. At her left sat Herr Schotte, the Assyriologist, whose features were effectually concealed by the convergence of his hair and beard, and whose glasses were continually falling into his plate. This gentleman had removed more tons of earth in the course of his explorations than had any of his confrères, and his vigorous attack upon his food seemed to suggest the strenuous nature of his accustomed toil. His eyes were small and deeply set, and his forehead bulged fiercely above his eyes in a bony ridge. His heavy brows completed the leonine suggestion of his face. Even to Imogen, who knew something of his work and greatly respected it, he was entirely too reminiscent of the stone age to be altogether an agreeable dinner companion. He seemed, indeed, to have absorbed something of the savagery of those early types of life which he continually studied.

Frank Wellington, the young Kansas man who had been two years out of Harvard and had published three historical novels, sat next to Mr. Will Maidenwood, who was still pale from his recent sufferings, and carried his hand bandaged. They took little part in the general conversation, but, like the lion and the unicorn, were always at it; discussing, every time they met, whether there were or were not passages in Mr. Wellington's works which should be eliminated, out of consideration for the Young Person. Wellington had fallen into the hands of a great American syndicate which most effectually befriended struggling authors whose struggles were in the right direction, and which had guaranteed to make him famous before he was thirty. Feeling the security of his position, he stoutly defended those passages which jarred upon the sensitive nerves of the young editor of *Woman*. Maidenwood, in the smoothest of voices, urged the necessity of the author's recognizing certain restrictions at the outset, and Miss Broadwood, who joined the argument quite without invitation or encouragement, seconded him with pointed and malicious remarks which caused the young editor manifest discomfort. Restzhoff, the chemist, demanded the attention of the entire company for his exposition of his devices for manufacturing ice-cream from vegetable oils, and for administering drugs in bonbons.

Flavia, always noticeably restless at dinner, was somewhat apathetic toward the advocate of peptonized chocolate, and was plainly concerned about the sudden departure of M. Roux, who had announced that it would be necessary for him to leave to-morrow. M. Emile Roux, who sat at Flavia's right, was a man in middle life and quite bald, clearly without personal vanity, though his publishers preferred to circulate only those of his portraits taken in his ambrosial youth. Imogen was considerably shocked at his unlikeness to the slender, black-stocked Rolla he had looked at twenty. He had declined into the florid, settled heaviness of indifference and approaching age. There was, however, a certain look of durability and solidity about him; the look of a man who has earned the right to be fat and bald, and even silent at dinner if he chooses.

Throughout the discussion between Wellington and Will Maidenwood, though they invited his participation, he remained silent, betraying no sign either of interest or contempt. Since his arrival he had directed most of his conversation to Hamilton, who had never read one of his twelve great novels. This perplexed and troubled Flavia. On the night of his arrival, Jules Martel had enthusiastically declared, "There are schools and schools, manners and manners; but Roux is Roux, and Paris sets its watches by his clock." Flavia had already repeated this remark to Imogen. It haunted her, and each time she quoted it she was impressed anew.

Flavia shifted the conversation uneasily, evidently exasperated and excited by her repeated failures to draw the novelist out. "Monsieur Roux," she began abruptly, with her most animated smile, "I remember so well a statement I read some years ago in your 'Mes Etudes des Femmes,' to the effect that you have never met a really intelligent woman. May I ask, without being impertinent, whether that assertion still represents your experience?"

"I meant, madam," said the novelist conservatively, "intellectual in a sense very special, as we say of men in whom the purely intellectual functions seem almost independent."

"And you still think a woman so constituted a mythical

personage?" persisted Flavia, nodding her head encouragingly.

"*Une Méduse,* madam, who, if she were discovered, would transmute us all into stone," said the novelist, bowing gravely. "If she existed at all," he added deliberately, "it was my business to find her, and she has cost me many a vain pilgrimage. Like Rudel of Tripoli, I have crossed seas and penetrated deserts to seek her out. I have, indeed, encountered women of learning whose industry I have been compelled to respect; many who have possessed beauty and charm and perplexing cleverness; a few with remarkable information, and a sort of fatal facility."

"And Mrs. Browning, George Eliot, and your own Mme. Dudevant?" queried Flavia with that fervid enthusiasm with which she could, on occasion, utter things simply incomprehensible for their banality—at her feats of this sort Miss Broadwood was wont to sit breathless with admiration.

"Madam, while the intellect was undeniably present in the performances of those women, it was only the stick of the rocket. Although this woman has eluded me, I have studied her conditions and perturbations as astronomers conjecture the orbits of planets they have never seen. If she exists, she is probably neither an artist nor a woman with a mission, but an obscure personage, with imperative intellectual needs, who absorbs rather than produces."

Flavia, still nodding nervously, fixed a strained glance of interrogation upon M. Roux. "Then you think she would be a woman whose first necessity would be to know, whose instincts would be satisfied with only the best, who could draw from others; appreciative, merely?"

The novelist lifted his dull eyes to his interlocutress with an untranslatable smile, and a slight inclination of his shoulders. "Exactly so; you are really remarkable, madam," he added, in a tone of cold astonishment.

After dinner the guests took their coffee in the music-room, where Schemetzkin sat down at the piano to drum rag-time, and give his celebrated imitation of the boarding-school girl's execution of Chopin. He flatly refused to play anything more serious, and would practise only in the morning, when he had the music-room to himself. Hamilton and M. Roux repaired to the smoking-room to discuss the necessity of extending the tax on manufactured articles in France,—one of those conversations which particularly exasperated Flavia.

After Schemetzkin had grimaced and tortured the keyboard with malicious vulgarities for half an hour, Signor Donati, to put an end to his torture, consented to sing, and Flavia and Imogen went to fetch Arthur to play his accompaniments. Hamilton rose with an annoyed look, and placed his cigarette on the mantel. "Why yes, Flavia, I'll accompany him, provided he sings something with a melody, Italian arias or ballads, and provided the recital is not interminable."

"You will join us, M. Roux?"

"Thank you, but I have some letters to write," replied the novelist, bowing.

As Flavia had remarked to Imogen, "Arthur really played accompaniments remarkably well." To hear him recalled vividly the days of her childhood, when he always used to spend his business vacations at her mother's home in Maine. He had possessed for her that almost hypnotic influence which young men sometimes exert upon little girls. It was a sort of phantom love affair, subjective and fanciful, a precocity of instinct, like that tender and maternal concern which some little girls feel for their dolls. Yet this childish infatuation is capable of all the depressions and exaltations of love itself; it has its bitter jealousies, cruel disappointments, its exacting caprices.

Summer after summer she had awaited his coming and wept at his departure, indifferent to the gayer young men who had called her their sweetheart, and laughed at everything she said. Although Hamilton never said so, she had been always quite sure that he was fond of her. When he pulled her up the river to hunt for fairy knolls shut about by low, hanging willows, he was often silent for an hour at a time, yet she never felt that he was bored or was neglecting her. He would lie in the sand smoking, his eyes half closed, watching her play and she was always conscious that she was entertaining him. Sometimes he would take a copy of "Alice in Wonderland" in his pocket, and no one could read it as he could, laughing at her with his dark eyes, when anything amused him. No one else could laugh so, with just their eyes, and without moving a muscle of their face. Though he usually smiled at passages that seemed not at all funny to the child, she always laughed gleefully, because he was so seldom moved to mirth that any such demonstration delighted her and she took the credit of it entirely to herself. Her own inclination had been for serious stories, with sad endings, like the Little Mermaid, which he had once told her in an unguarded moment when she had a cold, and was put to bed early on her birthday night and cried because she could not have her party. But he highly disapproved of this preference, and had called it a morbid taste, and always shook his finger at her when she asked for the story. When she had been particularly good, or particularly neglected by other people, then he would sometimes melt and tell her the story, and never laugh at her if she enjoyed the "sad ending" even to tears. When Flavia had taken him away and he came no more, she wept inconsolably for the space of two weeks, and refused to learn her lessons. Then she found the story of the Little Mermaid herself, and forgot him.

Imogen had discovered at dinner that he could still smile at one secretly, out of his eyes, and that he had the old manner of outwardly seeming bored, but letting you know that he was not. She was intensely curious about his exact state of feeling toward his wife, and more curious still to catch a sense of his final adjustment to the conditions of life in general. This, she could not help feeling, she might get again—if she could have him alone for an hour, in some place where there was a little river and a sandy cover bordered by drooping willows, and a blue sky seen through white sycamore boughs.

That evening, before retiring, Flavia entered her husband's room, where he sat in his smoking-jacket, in one of his favourite low chairs.

"I suppose it's a grave responsibility to bring an ardent, serious young thing like Imogen here among all these fascinating personages," she remarked reflectively. "But, after all, one can never tell. These grave, silent girls have their own charm, even for facile people."

"O, so that is your plan?" queried her husband dryly. "I was wondering why you got her up here. She doesn't seem to mix well with the faciles. At least, so it struck me."

Flavia paid no heed to this jeering remark, but repeated, "No, after all, it may not be a bad thing."

"Then do consign her to that shaken reed, the tenor," said her husband yawning. "I remember she used to have a taste for the pathetic."

"And then," remarked Flavia coquettishly, "after all, I owe her mother a return in kind. She was not afraid to trifle with destiny."

But Hamilton was asleep in his chair.

Next morning Imogen found only Miss Broadwood in the breakfast-room.

"Good-morning, my dear girl, whatever are you doing up so early? They never breakfast before eleven. Most of them take their coffee in their room. Take this place by me."

Miss Broadwood looked particularly fresh and encouraging in her blue serge walking-skirt, her open jacket displaying an expanse of stiff, white, shirt bosom, dotted with some almost imperceptible figure and a dark blue-and-white neck-tie, neatly knotted under her wide, rolling collar. She wore a white rosebud in the lapel of her coat, and decidedly she seemed more than ever like a nice, clean boy on his holiday. Imogen was just hoping that they would breakfast alone when Miss Broadwood exclaimed, "Ah, there comes Arthur with the children. That's the reward of early rising in this house; you never get to see the youngsters at any other time."

Hamilton entered, followed by two dark, handsome little boys. The girl, who was very tiny, blond like her mother, and exceedingly frail, he carried in his arms. The boys came up and said good-morning with an ease and cheerfulness uncommon, even in well-bred children, but the little girl hid her face on her father's shoulder.

"She's a shy little lady," he explained, as he put her gently down in her chair. "I'm afraid she's like her father; she can't seem to get used to meeting people. And you, Miss Willard, did you dream of the white rabbit or the little mermaid?"

"O, I dreamed of them all! All the personages of that buried civilization," cried Imogen, delighted that his estranged manner of the night before had entirely vanished, and feeling that, somehow, the old confidential relations had been restored during the night.

"Come, William," said Miss Broadwood, turning to the younger of the two boys, "and what did you dream about?"

"We dreamed," said William gravely—he was the more assertive of the two and always spoke for both—"we dreamed that there were fireworks hidden in the basement of the carriage-house; lots and lots of fireworks."

His elder brother looked up at him with apprehensive astonishment, while Miss Broadwood hastily put her napkin to her lips, and Hamilton dropped his eyes. "If little boys dream things, they are so apt not to come true," he reflected sadly. This shook even the redoubtable William, and he glanced nervously at his brother. "But do things vanish just because they have been dreamed?" he objected.

"Generally that is the very best reason for their vanishing," said Arthur gravely.

"But, father, people can't help what they dream," remonstrated Edward gently.

"Oh, come! You're making these children talk like a Maeterlinck dialogue," laughed Miss Broadwood.

Flavia presently entered, a book in her hand, and bade them all good-morning. "Come, little people, which story shall it be this morning?" she asked winningly. Greatly excited, the children followed her into the garden. "She does then, sometimes," murmured Imogen as they left the breakfast-room.

"Oh, yes, to be sure," said Miss Broadwood cheerfully. "She reads a story to them every morning in the most picturesque part of the garden. The mother of the Gracchi, you know. She does so long, she says, for the time when they will be intellectual companions for her. What do you say to a walk over the hills?"

As they left the house they met Frau Lichtenfeld and the bushy Herr Schotte—the professor cut an astonishing figure in golf stockings—returning from a walk and engaged in an animated conversation on the tendencies of German fiction.

"Aren't they the most attractive little children," exclaimed Imogen as they wound down the road toward the river.

"Yes, and you must not fail to tell Flavia that you think so. She will look at you in a sort of startled way and say, 'Yes, aren't they?' and maybe she will go off and hunt them up and have tea with them, to fully appreciate them. She is awfully afraid of missing anything good, is Flavia. The way those youngsters manage to conceal their guilty presence in the House of Song is a wonder."

"But don't any of the artist-folk fancy children?" asked Imogen.

"Yes, they just fancy them and no more. The chemist remarked the other day that children are like certain salts which need not be actualized because the formulæ are quite sufficient for practical purposes. I don't see how even Flavia can endure to have that man about."

"I have always been rather curious to know what Arthur thinks of it all," remarked Imogen cautiously.

"Thinks of it!" ejaculated Miss Broadwood. "Why, my dear, what would any man think of having his house turned into a hotel, habited by freaks who discharge his servants, borrow his money, and insult his neighbours? This place is shunned like a lazaretto!"

"Well, then, why does he—why does he—" persisted Imogen.

"Bah!" interrupted Miss Broadwood impatiently, "why did he in the first place? That's the question."

"Marry her, you mean?" said Imogen, colouring.

"Exactly so," said Miss Broadwood sharply, as she snapped the lid of her match-box.

"I suppose that is a question rather beyond us, and certainly one which we cannot discuss," said Imogen. "But his toleration on this one point puzzles me, quite apart from other complications."

"Toleration? Why this point, as you call it, simply *is* Flavia. Who could conceive of her without it? I don't know where it's all going to end, I'm sure, and I'm equally sure that, if it were not for Arthur, I shouldn't care," declared Miss Broadwood, drawing her shoulders together.

"But will it end at all, now?"

"Such an absurd state of things can't go on indefinitely. A man isn't going to see his wife make a guy of herself forever, is he? Chaos has already begun in the servants' quarters. There are six different languages spoken there now. You see, it's on an entirely false basis. Flavia hasn't the slightest notion of what these people are really like, their good and their bad alike escape her. They, on the other hand, can't imagine what she is driving at. Now, Arthur is worse off than either faction; he is not in the fairy story in that he sees these people exactly as they are, *but* he is utterly unable to see Flavia as they see her. There you have the situation. Why can't he see her as we do? My dear, that has kept me awake o' nights. This man who has thought so much and lived so much, who is naturally a critic, really takes Flavia at very nearly her own estimate. But now I am entering upon a wilderness. From a brief acquaintance with her, you can know nothing of the icy fastnesses of Flavia's self-esteem. It's like St. Peter's; you can't realize its magnitude at once. You have to grow into a sense of it by living under its shadow. It has perplexed even Emile Roux, that merciless dissector of egoism. She has puzzled him the more because he saw at a glance what some of them do not perceive at once, and what will be mercifully concealed from Arthur until the trump sounds; namely, that all Flavia's artists have done or ever will do means exactly as much to her as a symphony means to an oyster; that there is no bridge by which the significance of any work of art could be conveyed to her."

"Then, in the name of goodness, why does she bother?" gasped Imogen. "She is pretty, wealthy, well-established; why should she bother?"

"That's what M. Roux has kept asking himself. I can't pretend to analyse it. She reads papers on the Literary

Landmarks of Paris, and the Loves of the Poets, and that sort of thing to clubs out in Chicago. To Flavia it is more necessary to be called clever than to breathe. I would give a good deal to know that glum Frenchman's diagnosis. He has been watching her out of those fishy eyes of his as a biologist watches a hemisphereless frog."

For several days after M. Roux's departure, Flavia gave an embarrassing share of her attention to Imogen. Embarrassing, because Imogen had the feeling of being energetically and futilely explored, she knew not for what. She felt herself under the globe of an air pump, expected to yield up something. When she confined the conversation to matters of general interest, Flavia conveyed to her with some pique that her one endeavour in life had been to fit herself to converse with her friends upon those things which vitally interested them. "One has no right to accept their best from people unless one gives, isn't it so? I want to be able to give——!" she declared vaguely. Yet whenever Imogen strove to pay her tithes, and plunged bravely into her plans for study next winter, Flavia grew absent-minded and interrupted her by amazing generalizations or by such embarrassing questions as, "And these grim studies really have charm for you; you are quite buried in them; they make other things seem light and ephemeral?"

"I rather feel as though I had got in here under false pretences," Imogen confided to Miss Broadwood, "I'm sure I don't know what it is that she wants of me."

"Ah," chuckled Jemima, "you are not equal to these heart to heart talks with Flavia. You utterly fail to communicate to her the atmosphere of that untroubled joy in which you dwell. You must remember that she gets no feeling out of things herself, and she demands that you impart yours to her by some process of psychic transmission. I once met a blind girl, blind from birth, who could discuss the peculiarities of the Barbizon school with just Flavia's glibness and enthusiasm. Ordinarily Flavia knows how to get what she wants from people, and her memory is wonderful. One evening I heard her giving Frau Lichtenfeld some random impressions about Hedda Gabler which she extracted from me five years ago; giving them with an impassioned conviction of which I was never guilty. But I have known other people who could appropriate your stories and opinions; Flavia is infinitely more subtle than that; she can soak up the very thrash and drift of your day dreams, and take the very thrills off your back as it were."

After some days of unsuccessful effort, Flavia withdrew herself, and Imogen found Hamilton ready to catch her when she was tossed a-field. He seemed only to have been awaiting this crisis, and at once their old intimacy reestablished itself as a thing inevitable and beautifully prepared for. She convinced herself that she had not been mistaken in him, despite all the doubts that had come up in later years, and this renewal of faith set more than one question thumping in her brain. "How did he, how can he?" she kept repeating with a tinge of her childish resentment. "What right had he to waste anything so fine?"

When Imogen and Arthur were returning from a walk before luncheon one morning about a week after M. Roux's departure, they noticed an absorbed group before one of the hall windows. Herr Schotte and Restzhoff sat on the window seat with a newspaper between them, while Wellington, Schemetzkin and Will Maidenwood looked over their shoulders. They seemed intensely interested, Herr Schotte occasionally pounding his knees with his fists in ebullitions of barbaric glee. When Imogen entered the hall, however, the men were all sauntering toward the breakfast-room and the paper was lying innocently on the divan. During luncheon the personnel of that window group were unwontedly animated and agreeable,—all save Schemetzkin, whose stare was blanker than ever, as though Roux's mantle of insulting indifference had fallen upon him, in addition to his own oblivious self absorption. Will Maidenwood seemed embarrassed and annoyed; the chemist employed himself with making polite speeches to Hamilton.— Flavia did not come down to lunch—and there was a malicious gleam under Herr Schotte's eyebrows. Frank Wellington announced nervously that an imperative letter from his protecting syndicate summoned him to the city.

After luncheon the men went to the golf links, and Imogen, at the first opportunity, possessed herself of the newspaper which had been left on the divan. One of the first things that caught her eye was an article headed "Roux on Tuft Hunters; The Advanced American Woman as He Sees Her; Aggressive, Superficial and Insincere." The entire interview was nothing more or less than a satiric characterization of Flavia, a-quiver with irritation and vitriolic malice. No one could mistake it; it was done with all his deftness of portraiture. Imogen had not finished the article when she heard a footstep, and clutching the paper she started precipitately toward the stairway as Arthur

entered. He put out his hand, looking critically at her dis-
tressed face.

"Wait a moment, Miss Willard," he said peremptorily, "I
want to see whether we can find what it was that so interested our friends this morning. Give me the paper, please."

Imogen grew quite white as he opened the journal. She
reached forward and crumpled it with her hands. "Please
don't, please don't," she pleaded, "it's something I don't
want you to see. Oh! why will you? It's just something low
and despicable that you can't notice."

Arthur had gently loosed her hands and he pointed her
to a chair. He lit a cigar and read the article through without comment. When he had finished it, he walked to the
fireplace, struck a match, and tossed the flaming journal
between the brass andirons.

"You are right," he remarked as he came back, dusting
his hands with his handkerchief. "It's quite impossible to
comment. There are extremes of blackguardism for which
we have no name. The only thing necessary is to see that
Flavia gets no wind of this. This seems to be my cue to act;
poor girl."

Imogen looked at him tearfully; she could only murmur,
"Oh, why did you read it!"

Hamilton laughed spiritlessly. "Come, don't you worry
about it. You always took other people's troubles too seriously. When you were little and all the world was gay and
everybody happy, you must needs get the Little Mermaid's
troubles to grieve over. Come with me into the music-
room. You remember the musical setting I once made you
for the Lay of the Jabberwock? I was trying it over the
other night, long after you were in bed, and I decided it

was quite as fine as the Erl-King music. How I wish I could give you some of the cake that Alice ate and make you a little girl again. Then, when you had got through the glass door into the little garden, you could call to me, perhaps, and tell me all the fine things that were going on there. What a pity it is that you ever grew up!" he added, laughing, and Imogen, too, was thinking just that.

At dinner that evening, Flavia, with fatal persistence, insisted upon turning the conversation to M. Roux. She had been reading one of his novels and had remembered anew that Paris set its watches by his clock. Imogen surmised that she was tortured by a feeling that she had not sufficiently appreciated him while she had had him. When she first mentioned his name, she was answered only by the pall of silence that fell over the company. Then every one began to talk at once, as though to correct a false position. They spoke of him with a fervid, defiant admiration, with the sort of hot praise that covers a double purpose. Imogen fancied she could see that they felt a kind of relief at what the man had done, even those who despised him for doing it; that they felt a spiteful heat against Flavia, as though she had tricked them, and a certain contempt for themselves that they had been beguiled. She was reminded of the fury of the crowd in the fairy tale, when once the child had called out that the king was in his night-clothes. Surely these people knew no more about Flavia than they had known before, but the mere fact that the thing had been said, altered the situation. Flavia, meanwhile, sat chattering amiably, pathetically unconscious of her nakedness.

Hamilton lounged, fingering the stem of his wine glass, gazing down the table at one face after another and study-

ing the various degrees of self-consciousness they exhibited. Imogen's eyes followed his, fearfully. When a lull came
in the spasmodic flow of conversation, Arthur, leaning back
in his chair, remarked deliberately, "As for M. Roux, his
very profession places him in that class of men whom society has never been able to accept unconditionally because
it has never been able to assume that they have any ordered
notion of taste. He and his ilk remain, with the mounte-
banks and snake charmers, people indispensable to our civilization, but wholly unreclaimed by it; people whom we
receive, but whose invitations we do not accept."

Fortunately for Flavia, this mine was not exploded until
just before the coffee was brought. Her laughter was pitiful
to hear; it echoed through the silent room as in a vault,
while she made some tremulously light remark about her
husband's drollery, grim as a jest from the dying. No one
responded and she sat nodding her head like a mechanical
toy and smiling her white, set smile through her teeth, until
Alcée Buisson and Frau Lichtenfeld came to her support.

After dinner the guests retired immediately to their
rooms, and Imogen went upstairs on tiptoe, feeling the
echo of breakage and the dust of crumbling in the air. She
wondered whether Flavia's habitual note of uneasiness were
not, in a manner, prophetic, and a sort of unconscious pre-
monition, after all. She sat down to write a letter, but she
found herself so nervous, her head so hot and her hands so
cold, that she soon abandoned the effort. Just as she was
about to seek Miss Broadwood, Flavia entered and
embraced her hysterically.

"My dearest girl," she began, "was there ever such an
unfortunate and incomprehensible speech made before?

Of course it is scarcely necessary to explain to you poor Arthur's lack of tact, and that he meant nothing. But they! Can they be expected to understand? He will feel wretchedly about it when he realizes what he has done, but in the meantime? And M. Roux, of all men! When we were so fortunate as to get him, and he made himself so unreservedly agreeable, and I fancied that, in his way, Arthur quite admired him. My dear, you have no idea what that speech has done. Schemetzkin and Herr Schotte have already sent me word that they must leave us to-morrow. Such a thing from a host!" Flavia paused, choked by tears of vexation and despair.

Imogen was thoroughly disconcerted; this was the first time she had ever seen Flavia betray any personal emotion which was indubitably genuine. She replied with what consolation she could. "Need they take it personally at all? It was a mere observation upon a class of people—"

"Which he knows nothing whatever about, and with whom he has no sympathy," interrupted Flavia. "Ah, my dear, you could not be *expected* to understand. You can't realize, knowing Arthur as you do, his entire lack of any æsthetic sense whatever. He is absolutely *nil,* stone deaf and stark blind, on that side. He doesn't mean to be brutal, it is just the brutality of utter ignorance. They always feel it—they are so sensitive to unsympathetic influences, you know; they know it the moment they come into the house. I have spent my life apologizing for him and struggling to conceal it; but in spite of me, he wounds them; his very attitude, even in silence, offends them. Heavens! do I not know, is it not perpetually and forever wounding me?

But there has never been anything so dreadful as this, never! If I could conceive of any possible motive, even!"

"But, surely, Mrs. Hamilton, it was, after all, a mere expression of opinion, such as we are any of us likely to venture upon any subject whatever. It was neither more personal nor more extravagant than many of M. Roux's remarks."

"But, Imogen, certainly M. Roux has the right. It is a part of his art, and that is altogether another matter. Oh, this is not the only instance!" continued Flavia passionately, "I've always had this narrow, bigoted prejudice to contend with. It has always held me back. But this—!"

"I think you mistake his attitude," replied Imogen, feeling a flush that made her ears tingle, "that is, I fancy he is more appreciative than he seems. A man can't be very demonstrative about those things—not if he is a real man. I should not think you would care much about saving the feelings of people who are too narrow to admit of any other point of view than their own." She stopped, finding herself in the impossible position of attempting to explain Hamilton to his wife; a task which, if once begun, would necessitate an entire course of enlightenment which she doubted Flavia's ability to receive, and which she could offer only with very poor grace.

"That's just where it stings most," here Flavia began pacing the floor, "it is just because they have all shown such tolerance, and have treated Arthur with such unfailing consideration, that I can find no reasonable pretext for his rancour. How can he fail to see the value of such friendships on the children's account, if for nothing else! What

an advantage for them to grow up among such associations! Even though he cares nothing about these things
himself he might realize that. Is there nothing I could say
by way of explanation? To them, I mean? If some one
were to explain to them how unfortunately limited he is in
these things—"

"I'm afraid I cannot advise you," said Imogen decidedly,
"but that, at least, seems to be impossible."

Flavia took her hand and glanced at her affectionately,
nodding nervously. "Of course, dear girl, I can't ask you to
be quite frank with me. Poor child, you are trembling and
your hands are icy. Poor Arthur! But you must not judge
him by this altogether; think how much he misses in life.
What a cruel shock you've had. I'll send you some sherry.
Good night, my dear."

When Flavia shut the door, Imogen burst into a fit of
nervous weeping.

Next morning she awoke after a troubled and restless
night. At eight o'clock Miss Broadwood entered in a red
and white striped bath-robe.

"Up, up, and see the great doom's image!" she cried, her
eyes sparkling with excitement. "The hall is full of trunks,
they are packing. What bolt has fallen? It's you, *ma chérie,*
you've brought Ulysses home again and the slaughter has
begun!" She blew a cloud of smoke triumphantly from her
lips and threw herself into a chair beside the bed.

Imogen, rising on her elbow, plunged excitedly into the
story of the Roux interview, which Miss Broadwood heard
with the keenest interest, frequently interrupting her by
exclamations of delight. When Imogen reached the dramatic scene which terminated in the destruction of the

newspaper, Miss Broadwood rose and took a turn about the room, violently switching the tasselled cords of her bath-robe.

"Stop a moment," she cried, "you mean to tell me that he had such a heaven-sent means to bring her to her senses and didn't use it, that he held such a weapon and threw it away?"

"Use it?" cried Imogen unsteadily. "Of course he didn't! He bared his back to the tormentor, signed himself over to punishment in that speech he made at dinner, which every one understands but Flavia. She was here for an hour last night and disregarded every limit of taste in her maledictions."

"My dear!" cried Miss Broadwood, catching her hand in inordinate delight at the situation. "Do you see what he has done? There'll be no end to it. Why, he has sacrificed himself to spare the very vanity that devours him, put rancours in the vessels of his peace, and his eternal jewel given to the common enemy of man, to make them kings, the seed of Banquo kings! He is magnificent!"

"Isn't he always that?" cried Imogen hotly. "He's like a pillar of sanity and law in this house of shams and swollen vanities, where people stalk about with a sort of madhouse dignity, each one fancying himself a king or a pope. If you could have heard that woman talk of him! Why, she thinks him stupid, bigoted, blinded by middle-class prejudices. She talked about his having no æsthetic sense, and insisted that her artists had always shown him tolerance. I don't know why it should get on my nerves so, I'm sure, but her stupidity and assurance are enough to drive one to the brink of collapse."

"Yes, as opposed to his singular fineness, they are calculated to do just that," said Miss Broadwood gravely, wisely ignoring Imogen's tears. "But what has been is nothing to what will be. Just wait until Flavia's black swans have flown! You ought not to try to stick it out; that would only make it harder for every one. Suppose you let me telephone your mother to wire you to come home by the evening train?"

"Anything, rather than have her come at me like that again. It puts me in a perfectly impossible position, and he *is* so fine!"

"Of course it does," said Miss Broadwood sympathetically, "and there is no good to be got from facing it. I will stay, because such things interest me, and Frau Lichtenfeld will stay because she has no money to get away, and Buisson will stay because he feels somewhat responsible. These complications are interesting enough to cold-blooded folk like myself who have an eye for the dramatic element, but they are distracting and demoralizing to young people with any serious purpose in life."

Miss Broadwood's counsel was all the more generous seeing that, for her, the most interesting element of this dénouement would be eliminated by Imogen's departure. "If she goes now, she'll get over it," soliloquized Miss Broadwood, "if she stays she'll be wrung for him, and the hurt may go deep enough to last. I haven't the heart to see her spoiling things for herself." She telephoned Mrs. Willard, and helped Imogen to pack. She even took it upon herself to break the news of Imogen's going to Arthur, who remarked, as he rolled a cigarette in his nerveless fingers:

"Right enough, too. What should she do here with old cynics like you and me, Jimmy? Seeing that she is brim full of dates and formulæ and other positivisms, and is so girt about with illusions that she still casts a shadow in the sun. You've been very tender of her, haven't you? I've watched you. And to think it may all be gone when we see her next. 'The common fate of all things rare,' you know. What a good fellow you are, anyway, Jimmy," he added, putting his hands affectionately on her shoulders.

Arthur went with them to the station. Flavia was so prostrated by the concerted action of her guests that she was able to see Imogen only for a moment in her darkened sleeping chamber, where she kissed her hysterically, without lifting her head, bandaged in aromatic vinegar. On the way to the station both Arthur and Imogen threw the burden of keeping up appearances entirely upon Miss Broadwood, who blithely rose to the occasion. When Hamilton carried Imogen's bag into the car, Miss Broadwood detained her for a moment, whispering as she gave her a large, warm handclasp, "I'll come to see you when I get back to town; and, in the meantime, if you meet any of our artists, tell them you have left Caius Marius among the ruins of Carthage."

from O PIONEERS!

One Sunday afternoon in July, six months after John Bergson's death, Carl was sitting in the doorway of the Linstrum kitchen, dreaming over an illustrated paper, when he heard the rattle of a wagon along the hill road. Looking up he recognized the Bergsons' team, with two seats in the wagon, which meant they were off for a pleasure excursion. Oscar and Lou, on the front seat, wore their cloth hats and coats, never worn except on Sundays, and Emil, on the second seat with Alexandra, sat proudly in his new trousers, made from a pair of his father's, and a pink-striped shirt, with a wide ruffled collar. Oscar stopped the horses and waved to Carl, who caught up his hat and ran through the melon patch to join them.

"Want to go with us?" Lou called. "We're going to Crazy Ivar's to buy a hammock."

"Sure." Carl ran up panting, and clambering over the wheel sat down beside Emil. "I've always wanted to see Ivar's pond. They say it's the biggest in all the country. Aren't you afraid to go to Ivar's in that new shirt, Emil? He might want it and take it right off your back."

Emil grinned. "I'd be awful scared to go," he admitted, "if you big boys weren't along to take care of me. Did you ever hear him howl, Carl? People say sometimes he runs about the country howling at night because he is afraid the Lord will destroy him. Mother thinks he must have done something awful wicked."

Lou looked back and winked at Carl. "What would you do, Emil, if you was out on the prairie by yourself and seen him coming?"

Emil stared. "Maybe I could hide in a badger-hole," he suggested doubtfully.

"But suppose there wasn't any badger-hole," Lou persisted. "Would you run?"

"No, I'd be too scared to run," Emil admitted mournfully, twisting his fingers. "I guess I'd sit right down on the ground and say my prayers."

The big boys laughed, and Oscar brandished his whip over the broad backs of the horses.

"He wouldn't hurt you, Emil," said Carl persuasively. "He came to doctor our mare when she ate green corn and swelled up most as big as the water-tank. He petted her just like you do your cats. I couldn't understand much he said, for he don't talk any English, but he kept patting her and groaning as if he had the pain himself, and saying, 'There now, sister, that's easier, that's better!' "

Lou and Oscar laughed, and Emil giggled delightedly and looked up at his sister.

"I don't think he knows anything at all about doctoring," said Oscar scornfully. "They say when horses have distemper he takes the medicine himself, and then prays over the horses."

Alexandra spoke up. "That's what the Crows said, but he cured their horses, all the same. Some days his mind is cloudy, like. But if you can get him on a clear day, you can learn a great deal from him. He understands animals. Didn't I see him take the horn off the Berquists' cow when she had torn it loose and went crazy? She was tearing all over the place, knocking herself against things. And at last she ran out on the roof of the old dugout and her legs went through and there she stuck, bellowing. Ivar came running with his white bag, and the moment he got to her she was quiet and let him saw her horn off and daub the place with tar."

Emil had been watching his sister, his face reflecting the sufferings of the cow. "And then didn't it hurt her any more?" he asked.

Alexandra patted him. "No, not any more. And in two days they could use her milk again."

The road to Ivar's homestead was a very poor one. He had settled in the rough country across the county line, where no one lived but some Russians,—half a dozen families who dwelt together in one long house, divided off like barracks. Ivar had explained his choice by saying that the fewer neighbors he had, the fewer temptations. Nevertheless, when one considered that his chief business was horse-doctoring, it seemed rather short-sighted of him to live in the most inaccessible place he could find. The Bergson wagon lurched along over the rough hummocks and grass banks, followed the bottom of winding draws, or skirted the margin of wide lagoons, where the golden coreopsis grew up out of the clear water and the wild ducks rose with a whirr of wings.

Lou looked after them helplessly. "I wish I'd brought my gun, anyway, Alexandra," he said fretfully. "I could have hidden it under the straw in the bottom of the wagon."

"Then we'd have had to lie to Ivar. Besides, they say he can smell dead birds. And if he knew, we would n't get anything out of him, not even a hammock. I want to talk to him, and he won't talk sense if he's angry. It makes him foolish."

Lou sniffed. "Whoever heard of him talking sense, anyhow! I'd rather have ducks for supper than Crazy Ivar's tongue."

Emil was alarmed. "Oh, but, Lou, you don't want to make him mad! He might howl!"

They all laughed again, and Oscar urged the horses up the crumbling side of a clay blank. They had left the lagoons and the red grass behind them. In Crazy Ivar's country the grass was short and gray, the draws deeper than they were in the Bergsons' neighborhood, and the land was all broken up into hillocks and clay ridges. The wildflowers disappeared, and only in the bottom of the draws and gullies grew a few of the very toughest and hardiest: shoestring, and ironweed, and snow-on-the-mountain.

"Look, look, Emil, there's Ivar's big pond!" Alexandra pointed to a shining sheet of water that lay at the bottom of a shallow draw. At one end of the pond was an earthen dam, planted with green willow bushes, and above it a door and a single window were set into the hillside. You would not have seen them at all but for the reflection of the sunlight upon the four panes of window-glass. And that was all you saw. Not a shed, not a corral, not a well, not even a path broken in the curly grass. But for the piece of rusty stovepipe sticking up through the sod, you could have walked over the roof of Ivar's dwelling without dreaming that you were near a human habitation. Ivar had lived for three years in the clay bank, without defiling the face of nature any more than the coyote that had lived there before him had done.

When the Bergsons drove over the hill, Ivar was sitting in the doorway of his house, reading the Norwegian Bible. He was a queerly shaped old man, with a thick, powerful body set on short bow-legs. His shaggy white hair, falling in a thick mane about his ruddy cheeks, made him look older than he was. He was barefoot, but he wore a clean shirt of unbleached cotton, open at the neck. He always put on a clean shirt when Sunday morning came round, though he never went to church. He had a peculiar religion of his own and could not get on with any of the denominations. Often he did not see anybody from one week's end to another. He kept a calendar, and every morning he checked off a day, so that he was never in any doubt as to which day of the week it was. Ivar hired himself out in threshing and corn-husking time, and he doctored sick animals when he was sent for. When he was at home, he made hammocks out of twine and committed chapters of the Bible to memory.

Ivar found contentment in the solitude he had sought out for himself. He disliked the litter of human dwellings: the broken food, the bits of broken china, the old wash-boilers and tea-kettles thrown into the sunflower patch. He preferred the cleanness and tidiness of the wild sod. He always said that the badgers had cleaner houses than people, and that when he took a housekeeper her name would be Mrs. Badger. He best expressed his preference for his wild homestead by saying that his Bible seemed truer to him there. If one stood in the doorway of his cave, and looked off at the rough land, the smiling sky, the curly grass white in the hot sunlight; if one listened to the rapturous song of the lark, the drumming of the quail, the burr of the locust against that vast silence, one understood what Ivar meant.

On this Sunday afternoon his face shone with happiness. He closed the book on his knee, keeping the place with his horny finger, and repeated softly:—

> He sendeth the springs into the valleys, which run
>   among the hills;
> They give drink to every beast of the field; the wild
>   asses quench their thirst.
> The trees of the Lord are full of sap; the cedars of
>   Lebanon which he hath planted;
> Where the birds make their nests: as for the stork, the
>   fir trees are her house.
> The high hills are a refuge for the wild goats; and the
>   rocks for the conies.

Before he opened his Bible again, Ivar heard the Bergsons' wagon approaching, and he sprang up and ran toward it.

"No guns, no guns!" he shouted, waving his arms distractedly.

"No, Ivar, no guns," Alexandra called reassuringly.

He dropped his arms and went up to the wagon, smiling amiably and looking at them out of his pale blue eyes.

"We want to buy a hammock, if you have one," Alexandra explained, "and my little brother, here, wants to see your big pond, where so many birds come."

Ivar smiled foolishly, and began rubbing the horses' noses and feeling about their mouths behind the bits. "Not many birds just now. A few ducks this morning; and some snipe come to drink. But there was a crane last week. She spent one night and came back the next evening. I don't know why. It is not her season, of course. Many of them go over in the fall. Then the pond is full of strange voices every night."

Alexandra translated for Carl, who looked thoughtful. "Ask him, Alexandra, if it is true that a sea gull came here once. I have heard so."

She had some difficulty in making the old man understand.

He looked puzzled at first, then smote his hands together as he remembered. "Oh, yes, yes! A big white bird with long wings and pink feet. My! What a voice she had! She came in the afternoon and kept flying about the pond and screaming until dark. She was in trouble of some sort, but I could not understand her. She was going over to the other ocean, maybe, and did not know how far it was. She was afraid of never getting there. She was more mournful than our birds here; she cried in the night. She saw the light from my window and darted up to it. Maybe she thought my house was a boat, she was such a wild thing. Next morning, when the sun rose, I went out to take her

food, but she flew up into the sky and went on her way."
Ivar ran his fingers through his thick hair. "I have many
strange birds stop with me here. They come from very far
away and are great company. I hope you boys never shoot
wild birds?"

Lou and Oscar grinned, and Ivar shook his bushy head.
"Yes, I know boys are thoughtless. But these wild things
are God's birds. He watches over them and counts them, as
we do our cattle; Christ says so in the New Testament."

"Now, Ivar," Lou asked, "may we water our horses at
your pond and give them some feed? It's a bad road to your
place."

"Yes, yes, it is." The old man scrambled about and began
to loose the tugs. "A bad road, eh, girls? And the bay with
a colt at home!"

Oscar brushed the old man aside. "We'll take care of the
horses, Ivar. You'll be finding some disease on them. Alexandra wants to see your hammocks."

Ivar led Alexandra and Emil to his little cave house. He
had but one room, neatly plastered and whitewashed, and
there was a wooden floor. There was a kitchen stove, a
table covered with oilcloth, two chairs, a clock, a calendar,
a few books on the window-shelf; nothing more. But the
place was as clean as a cupboard.

"But where do you sleep, Ivar?" Emil asked, looking
about.

Ivar unslung a hammock from a hook on the wall; in it
was rolled a buffalo robe. "There, my son. A hammock is a
good bed, and in winter I wrap up in this skin. Where I go
to work, the beds are not half so easy as this."

By this time Emil had lost all his timidity. He thought a

cave a very superior kind of house. There was something pleasantly unusual about it and about Ivar. "Do the birds know you will be kind to them, Ivar? Is that why so many come?" he asked.

Ivar sat down on the floor and tucked his feet under him. "See, little brother, they have come from a long way, and they are very tired. From up there where they are flying, our country looks dark and flat. They must have water to drink and to bathe in before they can go on with their journey. They look this way and that, and far below them they see something shining, like a piece of glass set in the dark earth. That is my pond. They come to it and are not disturbed. Maybe I sprinkle a little corn. They tell the other birds, and next year more come this way. They have their roads up there, as we have down here."

Emil rubbed his knees thoughtfully. "And is that true, Ivar, about the head ducks falling back when they are tired, and the hind ones taking their place?"

"Yes. The point of the wedge gets the worst of it; they cut the wind. They can only stand it there a little while— half an hour, maybe. Then they fall back and the wedge splits a little, while the rear ones come up the middle to the front. Then it closes up and they fly on, with a new edge. They are always changing like that, up in the air. Never any confusion; just like soldiers who have been drilled."

Alexandra had selected her hammock by the time the boys came up from the pond. They would not come in, but sat in the shade of the bank outside while Alexandra and Ivar talked about the birds and about his housekeeping, and why he never ate meat, fresh or salt.

Alexandra was sitting on one of the wooden chairs, her

arms resting on the table. Ivar was sitting on the floor at her feet. "Ivar," she said suddenly, beginning to trace the pattern on the oilcloth with her forefinger, "I came to-day more because I wanted to talk to you than because I wanted to buy a hammock."

"Yes?" The old man scraped his bare feet on the plank floor.

"We have a big bunch of hogs, Ivar. I would n't sell in the spring, when everybody advised me to, and now so many people are losing their hogs that I am frightened. What can be done?"

Ivar's little eyes began to shine. They lost their vagueness.

"You feed them swill and such stuff? Of course! And sour milk? Oh, yes! And keep them in a stinking pen? I tell you, sister, the hogs of this country are put upon! They become unclean, like the hogs in the Bible. If you kept your chickens like that, what would happen? You have a little sorghum patch, maybe? Put a fence around it, and turn the hogs in. Build a shed to give them shade, a thatch on poles. Let the boys haul water to them in barrels, clean water, and plenty. Get them off the old stinking ground, and do not let them go back there until winter. Give them only grain and clean feed, such as you would give horses or cattle. Hogs do not like to be filthy."

The boys outside the door had been listening. Lou nudged his brother. "Come, the horses are done eating. Let's hitch up and get out of here. He'll fill her full of notions. She'll be for having the pigs sleep with us, next."

Oscar grunted and got up. Carl, who could not understand what Ivar said, saw that the two boys were displeased.

They did not mind hard work, but they hated experiments and could never see the use of taking pains. Even Lou, who was more elastic than his older brother, disliked to do anything different from their neighbors. He felt that it made them conspicuous and gave people a chance to talk about them.

Once they were on the homeward road, the boys forgot their ill-humor and joked about Ivar and his birds. Alexandra did not propose any reforms in the care of the pigs, and they hoped she had forgotten Ivar's talk. They agreed that he was crazier than ever, and would never be able to prove up on his land because he worked it so little. Alexandra privately resolved that she would have a talk with Ivar about this and stir him up. The boys persuaded Carl to stay for supper and go swimming in the pasture pond after dark.

That evening, after she had washed the supper dishes, Alexandra sat down on the kitchen doorstep, while her mother was mixing the bread. It was a still, deep-breathing summer night, full of the smell of the hay fields. Sounds of laughter and splashing came up from the pasture, and when the moon rose rapidly above the bare rim of the prairie, the pond glittered like polished metal, and she could see the flash of white bodies as the boys ran about the edge, or jumped into the water. Alexandra watched the shimmering pool dreamily, but eventually her eyes went back to the sorghum patch south of the barn, where she was planning to make her new pig corral.

from MY ÁNTONIA

One afternoon we were having our reading lesson on the warm, grassy bank where the badger lived. It was a day of amber sunlight, but there was a shiver of coming winter in the air. I had seen ice on the little horse-pond that morning, and as we went through the garden we found the tall asparagus, with its red berries, lying on the ground, a mass of slimy green.

Tony was barefooted, and she shivered in her cotton dress and was comfortable only when we were tucked down on the baked earth, in the full blaze of the sun. She could talk to me about almost anything by this time. That afternoon she was telling me how highly esteemed our friend the badger was in her part of the world, and how men kept a special kind of dog, with very short legs, to hunt him. Those dogs, she said, went down into the hole after the badger and killed him there in a terrific struggle underground; you could hear the barks and yelps outside. Then the dog dragged himself back, covered with bites and scratches, to be rewarded and petted by his master. She knew a dog who had a star on his collar for every badger he had killed.

The rabbits were unusually spry that afternoon. They kept starting up all about us, and dashing off down the draw as if they were playing a game of some kind. But the little buzzing things that lived in the grass were all dead—all but one. While we were lying there against the warm bank, a little insect of the palest, frailest green hopped painfully out of the buffalo grass and tried to leap into a bunch of bluestem. He missed it, fell back, and sat with his head sunk between his long legs, his antennae quivering, as if he were waiting for something to come and finish him. Tony made a warm nest for him in her hands; talked to him gaily and indulgently in Bohemian. Presently he began to sing for us—a thin, rusty little chirp. She held him close to her ear and laughed, but a moment afterward I saw there were tears in her eyes. She told me that in her village at home there was an old beggar woman who went about selling herbs and roots she had dug up in the forest. If you took her in and gave her a warm place by the fire, she sang old songs to the children in a cracked voice, like this. Old Hata, she was called, and the children loved to see her coming and saved their cakes and sweets for her.

When the bank on the other side of the draw began to throw a narrow shelf of shadow, we knew we ought to be starting homeward; the chill came on quickly when the sun got low, and Ántonia's dress was thin. What were we to do with the frail little creature we had lured back to life by false pretenses? I offered my pockets, but Tony shook her head and carefully put the green insect in her hair, tying her big handkerchief down loosely over her curls. I said I would go with her until we could see Squaw Creek, and then turn and run home. We drifted along lazily, very happy, through the magical light of the late afternoon.

All those fall afternoons were the same, but I never got used to them. As far as we could see, the miles of copper-red grass were drenched in sunlight that was stronger and fiercer than at any other time of the day. The blond corn-fields were red gold, the haystacks turned rosy and threw long shadows. The whole prairie was like the bush that burned with fire and was not consumed. That hour always had the exultation of victory, of triumphant ending, like a hero's death—heroes who died young and gloriously. It was a sudden transfiguration, a lifting-up of day.

How many an afternoon Ántonia and I have trailed along the prairie under that magnificence! And always two long black shadows flitted before us or followed after, dark spots on the ruddy grass.

We had been silent a long time, and the edge of the sun sank nearer and nearer the prairie floor, when we saw a figure moving on the edge of the upland, a gun over his shoulder. He was walking slowly, dragging his feet along as if he had no purpose. We broke into a run to overtake him.

"My papa sick all the time," Tony panted as we flew. "He not look good, Jim."

As we neared Mr. Shimerda she shouted, and he lifted his head and peered about. Tony ran up to him, caught his hand and pressed it against her cheek. She was the only one of his family who could rouse the old man from the torpor in which he seemed to live. He took the bag from his belt and showed us three rabbits he had shot, looked at Ántonia with a wintry flicker of a smile and began to tell her something. She turned to me.

"My *tatinek* make me little hat with the skins, little hat for winter!" she exclaimed joyfully. "Meat for eat, skin for hat"—she tolled off these benefits on her fingers.

Her father put his hand on her hair, but she caught his wrist and lifted it carefully away, talking to him rapidly. I heard the name of old Hata. He untied the handkerchief, separated her hair with his fingers, and stood looking down at the green insect. When it began to chirp faintly, he listened as if it were a beautiful sound.

I picked up the gun he had dropped; a queer piece from the old country, short and heavy, with a stag's head on the cock. When he saw me examining it, he turned to me with his faraway look that always made me feel as if I were down at the bottom of a well. He spoke kindly and gravely, and Ántonia translated:

"My *tatinek* say when you are big boy, he give you his gun. Very fine, from Bohemie. It was belong to a great man, very rich, like what you not got here; many fields, many forests, many big house. My papa play for his wedding, and he give my papa fine gun, and my papa give you."

I was glad that this project was one of futurity. There never were such people as the Shimerdas for wanting to give away everything they had. Even the mother was always offering me things, though I knew she expected substantial presents in return. We stood there in friendly silence, while the feeble minstrel sheltered in Ántonia's hair went on with its scratchy chirp. The old man's smile, as he listened, was so full of sadness, of pity for things, that I never afterward forgot it. As the sun sank there came a sudden coolness and the strong smell of earth and drying grass. Ántonia and her father went off hand in hand, and I buttoned up my jacket and raced my shadow home.

Much as I liked Ántonia, I hated a superior tone that she sometimes took with me. She was four years older than I, to be sure, and had seen more of the world; but I was a boy and she was a girl, and I resented her protecting manner. Before the autumn was over, she began to treat me more like an equal and to defer to me in other things than reading lessons. This change came about from an adventure we had together.

One day when I rode over to the Shimerdas' I found Ántonia starting off on foot for Russian Peter's house, to borrow a spade Ambrosch needed. I offered to take her on the pony, and she got up behind me. There had been another black frost the night before, and the air was clear and heady as wine. Within a week all the blooming roads had been despoiled, hundreds of miles of yellow sunflowers had been transformed into brown, rattling, burry stalks.

We found Russian Peter digging his potatoes. We were glad to go in and get warm by his kitchen stove and to see his squashes and Christmas melons, heaped in the store-room for winter. As we rode away with the spade, Ántonia suggested that we stop at the prairie-dog-town and dig into one of the holes. We could find out whether they ran straight down, or were horizontal, like mole-holes; whether they had underground connections; whether the owls had nests down there, lined with feathers. We might get some puppies, or owl eggs, or snakeskins.

The dog-town was spread out over perhaps ten acres. The grass had been nibbled short and even, so this stretch was not shaggy and red like the surrounding country, but grey and velvety. The holes were several yards apart, and were disposed with a good deal of regularity, almost as if the town had been laid out in streets and avenues. One always felt that an orderly and very sociable kind of life was going on there. I picketed Dude down in a draw, and we went wandering about, looking for a hole that would be easy to dig. The dogs were out, as usual, dozens of them, sitting up on their hind legs over the doors of their houses. As we approached, they barked, shook their tails at us, and scurried underground. Before the mouths of the holes were little patches of sand and gravel, scratched up, we supposed, from a long way below the surface. Here and there, in the town, we came on larger gravel patches, several yards away from any hole. If the dogs had scratched the sand up in excavating, how had they carried it so far? It was on one of these gravel beds that I met my adventure.

We were examining a big hole with two entrances. The burrow sloped into the ground at a gentle angle, so that we could see where the two corridors united, and the floor was dusty from use, like a little highway over which much travel went. I was walking backward, in a crouching position, when I heard Ántonia scream. She was standing opposite me, pointing behind me and shouting something in Bohemian. I whirled round, and there, on one of those dry gravel beds, was the biggest snake I had ever seen. He was sunning himself, after the cold night, and he must have been asleep when Ántonia screamed. When I turned, he was lying in long loose waves, like a letter "W." He twitched and began to coil slowly. He was not merely a big snake, I thought—he was a circus monstrosity. His abominable muscularity, his loathsome, fluid motion, somehow made me sick. He was as thick as my leg, and looked as if mill-stones couldn't crush the disgusting vitality out of him. He lifted his hideous little head, and rattled. I didn't run because I didn't think of it—if my back had been against a stone wall I couldn't have felt more cornered. I saw his coils tighten—now he would spring, spring his length, I remembered. I ran up and drove at his head with my spade, struck him fairly across the neck, and in a minute he was all about my feet in wavy loops. I struck now from hate. Ántonia, barefooted as she was, ran up behind me. Even after I had pounded his ugly head flat, his body kept on coiling and winding, doubling and falling back on itself. I walked away and turned my back. I felt seasick.

Ántonia came after me, crying, "O Jimmy, he not bite you? You sure? Why you not run when I say?"

"What did you jabber Bohunk for? You might have told me there was a snake behind me!" I said petulantly.

"I know I am just awful, Jim, I was so scared." She took my handkerchief from my pocket and tried to wipe my face with it, but I snatched it away from her. I suppose I looked as sick as I felt.

"I never know you was so brave, Jim," she went on comfortingly. "You is just like big mans; you wait for him lift his head and then you go for him. Ain't you feel scared a bit? Now we take that snake home and show everybody. Nobody ain't seen in this kawntree so big snake like you kill."

She went on in this strain until I began to think that I had longed for this opportunity, and had hailed it with joy. Cautiously we went back to the snake; he was still groping with his tail, turning up his ugly belly in the light. A faint, fetid smell came from him, and a thread of green liquid oozed from his crushed head.

"Look, Tony, that's his poison," I said.

I took a long piece of string from my pocket, and she lifted his head with the spade while I tied a noose around it. We pulled him out straight and measured him by my riding-quirt; he was about five and a half feet long. He had twelve rattles, but they were broken off before they began to taper, so I insisted that he must once have had twenty-four. I explained to Ántonia how this meant that he was twenty-four years old, that he must have been there when white men first came, left on from buffalo and Indian times. As I turned him over, I began to feel proud of him, to have a kind of respect for his age and size. He seemed like the ancient, eldest Evil. Certainly his kind have left horrible unconscious memories in all warm-blooded life. When we dragged him down into the draw, Dude sprang off to the end of his tether and shivered all over—wouldn't let us come near him.

We decided that Ántonia should ride Dude home, and I would walk. As she rode along slowly, her bare legs swinging against the pony's side, she kept shouting back to me about how astonished everybody would be. I followed with the spade over my shoulder, dragging my snake. Her exultation was contagious. The great land had never looked to me so big and free. If the red grass were full of rattlers, I was equal to them all. Nevertheless, I stole furtive glances behind me now and then to see that no avenging mate, older and bigger than my quarry, was racing up from the rear.

The sun had set when we reached our garden and went down the draw toward the house. Otto Fuchs was the first one we met. He was sitting on the edge of the cattle-pond, having a quiet pipe before supper. Ántonia called him to come quick and look. He did not say anything for a minute, but scratched his head and turned the snake over with his boot.

"Where did you run onto that beauty, Jim?"

"Up at the dog-town," I answered laconically.

"Kill him yourself? How come you to have a weapon?"

"We'd been up to Russian Peter's, to borrow a spade for Ambrosch."

Otto shook the ashes out of his pipe and squatted down to count the rattles. "It was just luck you had a tool," he said cautiously. "Gosh! I wouldn't want to do any business with that fellow myself, unless I had a fence-post along. Your grandmother's snake-cane wouldn't more than tickle him. He could stand right up and talk to you, he could. Did he fight hard?"

Ántonia broke in: "He fight something awful! He is all over Jimmy's boots. I scream for him to run, but he just hit and hit that snake like he was crazy."

Otto winked at me. After Ántonia rode on he said: "Got him in the head first crack, didn't you? That was just as well."

We hung him up to the windmill, and when I went down to the kitchen, I found Ántonia standing in the middle of the floor, telling the story with a great deal of colour.

Subsequent experiences with rattlesnakes taught me that

my first encounter was fortunate in circumstance. My big rattler was old, and had led too easy a life; there was not much fight in him. He had probably lived there for years, with a fat prairie-dog for breakfast whenever he felt like it, a sheltered home, even an owl-feather bed, perhaps, and he had forgot that the world doesn't owe rattlers a living. A snake of his size, in fighting trim, would be more than any boy could handle. So in reality it was a mock adventure; the game was fixed for me by chance, as it probably was for many a dragon-slayer. I had been adequately armed by Russian Peter; the snake was old and lazy; and I had Ántonia beside me, to appreciate and admire.

That snake hung on our corral fence for several days; some of the neighbours came to see it and agreed that it was the biggest rattler ever killed in those parts. This was enough for Ántonia. She liked me better from that time on, and she never took a supercilious air with me again. I had killed a big snake—I was now a big fellow.

COMING, APHRODITE!

I

Don Hedger had lived for four years on the top floor of an old house on the south side of Washington Square, and nobody had ever disturbed him. He occupied one big room with no outside exposure except on the north, where he had built in a many-paned studio window that looked upon a court and upon the roofs and walls of other buildings. His room was very cheerless, since he never got a ray of direct sunlight; the south corners were always in shadow. In one of the corners was a clothes closet, built against the partition, in another a wide divan, serving as a seat by day and a bed by night. In the front corner, the one farther from the window, was a sink, and a table with two gas burners where he sometimes cooked his food. There, too, in the perpetual dusk, was the dog's bed, and often a bone or two for his comfort.

The dog was a Boston bull terrier, and Hedger explained his surly disposition by the fact that he had been bred to the point where it told on his nerves. His name was Caesar III, and he had taken prizes at very exclusive dog shows. When he and his master went out to prowl about University Place or to promenade along West Street, Caesar III was invariably fresh and shining. His pink skin showed through his mottled coat, which glistened as if it had just been rubbed with olive oil, and he wore a brass-studded collar, bought at the smartest saddler's. Hedger, as often as not, was hunched up in an old striped blanket coat, with a shapeless felt hat pulled over his bushy hair, wearing black shoes that had become grey, or brown ones that had become black, and he never put on gloves unless the day was biting cold.

Early in May, Hedger learned that he was to have a new neighbour in the rear apartment—two rooms, one large and one small, that faced the west. His studio was shut off from the larger of these rooms by double doors, which, though they were fairly tight, left him a good deal at the mercy of the occupant. The rooms had been leased, long before he came there, by a trained nurse who considered herself knowing in old furniture. She went to auction sales and bought up mahogany and dirty brass and stored it away here, where she meant to live when she retired from nursing. Meanwhile, she sub-let her rooms, with their precious furniture, to young people who came to New York to "write" or to "paint"—who proposed to live by the sweat of the brow rather than of the hand, and who desired artistic surroundings. When Hedger first moved in, these rooms were occupied by a young man who tried to write plays,— and who kept on trying until a week ago, when the nurse had put him out for unpaid rent.

A few days after the playwright left, Hedger heard an

ominous murmur of voices through the bolted double doors: the lady-like intonation of the nurse—doubtless exhibiting her treasures—and another voice, also a woman's, but very different; young, fresh, unguarded, confident. All the same, it would be very annoying to have a woman in there. The only bath-room on the floor was at the top of the stairs in the front hall, and he would always be running into her as he came or went from his bath. He would have to be more careful to see that Caesar didn't leave bones about the hall, too; and she might object when he cooked steak and onions on his gas burner.

As soon as the talking ceased and the women left, he forgot them. He was absorbed in a study of paradise fish at the Aquarium, staring out at people through the glass and green water of their tank. It was a highly gratifying idea; the incommunicability of one stratum of animal life with another,—though Hedger pretended it was only an experiment in unusual lighting. When he heard trunks knocking against the sides of the narrow hall, then he realized that she was moving in at once. Toward noon, groans and deep gasps and the creaking of ropes, made him aware that a piano was arriving. After the tramp of the movers died away down the stairs, somebody touched off a few scales and chords on the instrument, and then there was peace. Presently he heard her lock her door and go down the hall humming something; going out to lunch, probably. He stuck his brushes in a can of turpentine and put on his hat, not stopping to wash his hands. Caesar was smelling along the crack under the bolted doors; his bony tail stuck out hard as a hickory withe, and the hair was standing up about his elegant collar.

Hedger encouraged him. "Come along, Caesar. You'll soon get used to a new smell."

In the hall stood an enormous trunk, behind the ladder that led to the roof, just opposite Hedger's door. The dog flew at it with a growl of hurt amazement. They went down three flights of stairs and out into the brilliant May afternoon.

Behind the Square, Hedger and his dog descended into a basement oyster house where there were no tablecloths on the tables and no handles on the coffee cups, and the floor was covered with sawdust, and Caesar was always welcome,—not that he needed any such precautionary flooring. All the carpets of Persia would have been safe for him. Hedger ordered steak and onions absentmindedly, not realizing why he had an apprehension that this dish might be less readily at hand hereafter. While he ate, Caesar sat beside his chair, gravely disturbing the sawdust with his tail.

After lunch Hedger strolled about the Square for the dog's health and watched the stages pull out;—that was almost the very last summer of the old horse stages on Fifth Avenue. The fountain had but lately begun operations for the season and was throwing up a mist of rainbow water which now and then blew south and sprayed a bunch of Italian babies that were being supported on the outer rim by older, very little older, brothers and sisters. Plump robins were hopping about on the soil; the grass was newly cut and blindingly green. Looking up the Avenue through the Arch, one could see the young poplars with their bright, sticky leaves, and the Brevoort glistening in its spring coat of paint, and shining horses and carriages,—occasionally an automobile, mis-shapen and sullen, like an ugly threat in a stream of things that were bright and beautiful and alive.

While Caesar and his master were standing by the fountain, a girl approached them, crossing the Square. Hedger noticed her because she wore a lavender cloth suit and carried in her arms a big bunch of fresh lilacs. He saw that she was young and handsome,—beautiful, in fact, with a splendid figure and good action. She, too, paused by the fountain and looked back through the Arch up the Avenue. She smiled rather patronizingly as she looked, and at the same time seemed delighted. Her slowly curving upper lip and half-closed eyes seemed to say: "You're gay, you're exciting, you are quite the right sort of thing; but you're none too fine for me!"

In the moment she tarried, Caesar stealthily approached her and sniffed at the hem of her lavender skirt, then, when she went south like an arrow, he ran back to his master and lifted a face full of emotion and alarm, his lower lip twitching under his sharp white teeth and his hazel eyes pointed with a very definite discovery. He stood thus, motionless, while Hedger watched the lavender girl go up the steps and through the door of the house in which he lived.

"You're right, my boy, it's she! She might be worse looking, you know."

When they mounted to the studio, the new lodger's door, at the back of the wall, was a little ajar, and Hedger caught the warm perfume of lilacs just brought in out of the sun. He was used to the musty smell of the old hall carpet. (The nurse-lessee had once knocked at his studio

door and complained that Caesar must be somewhat responsible for the particular flavour of that mustiness, and
Hedger had never spoken to her since.) He was used to
the old smell, and he preferred it to that of the lilacs, and
so did his companion, whose nose was so much more dis-
criminating. Hedger shut his door vehemently, and fell
to work.

Most young men who dwell in obscure studios in New
York have had a beginning, come out of something, have
somewhere a home town, a family, a paternal roof. But
Don Hedger had no such background. He was a foundling,
and had grown up in a school for homeless boys, where
book-learning was a negligible part of the curriculum.
When he was sixteen, a Catholic priest took him to Greens-
burg, Pennsylvania, to keep house for him. The priest did
something to fill in the large gaps in the boy's education,—
taught him to like "Don Quixote" and "The Golden Legend," and encouraged him to mess with paints and crayons
in his room up under the slope of the mansard. When Don
wanted to go to New York to study at the Art League, the
priest got him a night job as packer in one of the big
department stores. Since then, Hedger had taken care of
himself; that was his only responsibility. He was singularly
unencumbered; had no family duties, no social ties, no
obligations toward any one but his landlord. Since he travelled light, he had travelled rather far. He had got over a
good deal of the earth's surface, in spite of the fact that he
never in his life had more than three hundred dollars ahead
at any one time, and he had already outlived a succession of
convictions and revelations about his art.

Though he was not but twenty-six years old, he had

twice been on the verge of becoming a marketable product; once through some studies of New York streets he did for a magazine, and once through a collection of pastels he brought home from New Mexico, which Remington, then at the height of his popularity, happened to see, and generously tried to push. But on both occasions Hedger decided that this was something he didn't wish to carry further,—simply the old thing over again and got nowhere—so he took enquiring dealers experiments in a "later manner," that made them put him out of the shop. When he ran short of money, he could always get any amount of commercial work; he was an expert draughtsman and worked with lightning speed. The rest of his time he spent in groping his way from one kind of painting into another, or travelling about without luggage, like a tramp, and he was chiefly occupied with getting rid of ideas he had once thought very fine.

Hedger's circumstances, since he had moved to Washington Square, were affluent compared to anything he had ever known before. He was now able to pay advance rent and turn the key on his studio when he went away for four months at a stretch. It didn't occur to him to wish to be richer than this. To be sure, he did without a great many things other people think necessary, but he didn't miss them, because he had never had them. He belonged to no clubs, visited no houses, had no studio friends, and he ate his dinner alone in some decent little restaurant, even on Christmas and New Year's. For days together he talked to nobody but his dog and the janitress and the lame oysterman.

After he shut the door and settled down to his paradise fish on that first Tuesday in May, Hedger forgot all about his new neighbour. When the light failed, he took Caesar out for a walk. On the way home he did his marketing on West Houston Street, with a one-eyed Italian woman who always cheated him. After he had cooked his beans and scallopini, and drunk half a bottle of Chianti, he put his dishes in the sink and went up on the roof to smoke. He was the only person in the house who ever went to the roof, and he had a secret understanding with the janitress about it. He was to have "the privilege of the roof," as she said, if he opened the heavy trapdoor on sunny days to air out the upper hall, and was watchful to close it when rain threatened. Mrs. Foley was fat and dirty and hated to climb stairs,—besides, the roof was reached by a perpendicular iron ladder, definitely inaccessible to a woman of her bulk, and the iron door at the top of it was too heavy for any but Hedger's strong arm to lift. Hedger was not above medium height, but he practised with weights and dumb-bells, and in the shoulders he was as strong as a gorilla.

So Hedger had the roof to himself. He and Caesar often slept up there on hot nights, rolled in blankets he had brought home from Arizona. He mounted with Caesar under his left arm. The dog had never learned to climb a perpendicular ladder, and never did he feel so much his master's greatness and his own dependence upon him, as when he crept under his arm for this perilous ascent. Up there was even gravel to scratch in, and a dog could do whatever he liked, so long as he did not bark. It was a kind of heaven, which no one was strong enough to reach but his great, paint-smelling master.

On this blue May night there was a slender, girlish look-

ing young moon in the west, playing with a whole company of silver stars. Now and then one of them darted
away from the group and shot off into the gauzy blue with
a soft little trail of light, like laughter. Hedger and his dog
were delighted when a star did this. They were quite lost in
watching the glittering game, when they were suddenly
diverted by a sound,—not from the stars, though it was
music. It was not the Prologue to Pagliacci, which rose ever
and anon on hot evenings from an Italian tenement on
Thompson Street, with the gasps of the corpulent baritone
who got behind it; nor was it the hurdy-gurdy man, who
often played at the corner in the balmy twilight. No, this was
a woman's voice, singing the tempestuous, over-lapping
phrases of Signor Puccini, then comparatively new in the
world, but already so popular that even Hedger recognized
his unmistakable gusts of breath. He looked about over the
roofs; all was blue and still, with the well-built chimneys
that were never used now standing up dark and mournful.
He moved softly toward the yellow quadrangle where the
gas from the hall shone up through the half-lifted trapdoor.
Oh yes! It came up through the hole like a strong draught,
a big, beautiful voice, and it sounded rather like a professional's. A piano had arrived in the morning, Hedger
remembered. This might be a very great nuisance. It would
be pleasant enough to listen to, if you could turn it on and
off as you wished; but you couldn't. Caesar, with the gas
light shining on his collar and his ugly but sensitive face,
panted and looked up for information. Hedger put down a
reassuring hand.

"I don't know. We can't tell yet. It may not be so bad."

He stayed on the roof until all was still below, and finally descended, with quite a new feeling about his neighbour. Her voice, like her figure, inspired respect—if one did not choose to call it admiration. Her door was shut, the transom was dark; nothing remained of her but the obtrusive trunk, unrightfully taking up room in the narrow hall.

II

For two days Hedger didn't see her. He was painting eight hours a day just then, and only went out to hunt for food. He noticed that she practised scales and exercises for about an hour in the morning; then she locked her door, went humming down the hall, and left him in peace. He heard her getting her coffee ready at about the same time he got his. Earlier still, she passed his room on her way to her bath. In the evening she sometimes sang, but on the whole she didn't bother him. When he was working well he did not notice anything much. The morning paper lay before his door until he reached out for his milk bottle, then he kicked the sheet inside and it lay on the floor until evening. Sometimes he read it and sometimes he did not. He forgot there was anything of importance going on in the world outside of his third floor studio. Nobody had ever taught him that he ought to be interested in other people; in the Pittsburgh steel strike, in the Fresh Air Fund, in the scandal about the Babies' Hospital. A grey wolf, living in a Wyoming canyon, would hardly have been less concerned about these things than was Don Hedger.

One morning he was coming out of the bath-room at the front end of the hall, having just given Caesar his bath and rubbed him into a glow with a heavy towel. Before the door, lying in wait for him, as it were, stood a tall figure in a flowing blue silk dressing gown that fell away from her marble arms. In her hands she carried various accessories of the bath.

"I wish," she said distinctly, standing in his way, "I wish you wouldn't wash your dog in the tub. I never heard of such a thing! I've found his hair in the tub, and I've smelled a doggy smell, and now I've caught you at it. It's an outrage!"

Hedger was badly frightened. She was so tall and positive, and was fairly blazing with beauty and anger. He stood blinking, holding on to his sponge and dog-soap, feeling that he ought to bow very low to her. But what he actually said was:

"Nobody has ever objected before. I always wash the tub,—and, anyhow, he's cleaner than most people."

"Cleaner than me?" her eyebrows went up, her white arms and neck and her fragrant person seemed to scream at him like a band of outraged nymphs. Something flashed through his mind about a man who was turned into a dog, or was pursued by dogs, because he unwittingly intruded upon the bath of beauty.

"No, I didn't mean that," he muttered, turning scarlet under the bluish stubble of his muscular jaws. "But I know he's cleaner than I am."

"That I don't doubt!" Her voice sounded like a soft shivering of crystal, and with a smile of pity she drew the folds of her voluminous blue robe close about her and allowed the wretched man to pass. Even Caesar was frightened; he darted like a streak down the hall, through the door and to his own bed in the corner among the bones.

Hedger stood still in the doorway, listening to indignant sniffs and coughs and a great swishing of water about the sides of the tub. He had washed it; but as he had washed it with Caesar's sponge, it was quite possible that a few bristles remained; the dog was shedding now. The playwright had never objected, nor had the jovial illustrator who occupied the front apartment,—but he, as he admitted, "was usually pye-eyed, when he wasn't in Buffalo." He went home to Buffalo sometimes to rest his nerves.

It had never occurred to Hedger that anyone would mind using the tub after Caesar;—but then, he had never seen a beautiful girl caparisoned for the bath before. As soon as he beheld her standing there, he realized the unfitness of it. For that matter, she ought not to step into a tub that any other mortal had bathed in; the illustrator was sloppy and left cigarette ends on the moulding.

All morning as he worked he was gnawed by a spiteful desire to get back at her. It rankled that he had been so vanquished by her disdain. When he heard her locking her door to go out for lunch, he stepped quickly into the hall in his messy painting coat, and addressed her.

"I don't wish to be exigent, Miss,"—he had certain grand words that he used upon occasion—"but if this is your trunk, it's rather in the way here."

"Oh, very well!" she exclaimed carelessly, dropping her keys into her handbag. "I'll have it moved when I can get a man to do it," and she went down the hall with her free, roving stride.

Her name, Hedger discovered from her letters, which the postman left on the table in the lower hall, was Eden Bower.

III

In the closet that was built against the partition separating his room from Miss Bower's, Hedger kept all his wearing apparel, some of it on hooks and hangers, some of it on the floor. When he opened his closet door now-a-days, little dust-coloured insects flew out on downy wing, and he suspected that a brood of moths were hatching in his winter overcoat. Mrs. Foley, the janitress, told him to bring down all his heavy clothes and she would give them a beating and hang them in the court. The closet was in such disorder that he shunned the encounter, but one hot afternoon he set himself to the task. First he threw out a pile of forgotten laundry and tied it up in a sheet. The bundle stood as high as his middle when he had knotted the corners. Then he got his shoes and overshoes together. When he took his overcoat from its place against the partition, a long ray of yellow light shot across the dark enclosure,—a knot hole, evidently, in the high wainscoting of the west room. He had never noticed it before, and without realizing what he was doing, he stopped and squinted through it.

Yonder, in a pool of sunlight, stood his new neighbour, wholly unclad, doing exercises of some sort before a long gilt mirror. Hedger did not happen to think how unpardonable it was of him to watch her. Nudity was not improper to any one who had worked so much from the figure, and he continued to look, simply because he had never seen a woman's body so beautiful as this one,—positively glorious in action. As she swung her arms and changed from one pivot of motion to another, muscular energy seemed to flow through her from her toes to her finger-tips. The soft flush of exercise and the gold of afternoon sun played over her flesh together, enveloped her in a luminous mist which, as she turned and twisted, made now an arm, now a shoulder, now a thigh, dissolve in pure light and instantly recover its outline with the next gesture. Hedger's fingers curved as if he were holding a crayon; mentally he was doing the whole figure in a single running line, and the charcoal seemed to explode in his hand at the point where the energy of each gesture was discharged into the whirling disc of light, from a foot or shoulder, from the up-thrust chin or the lifted breasts.

He could not have told whether he watched her for six minutes or sixteen. When her gymnastics were over, she paused to catch up a lock of hair that had come down, and examined with solicitude a little reddish mole that grew under her left arm-pit. Then, with her hand on her hip, she walked unconcernedly across the room and disappeared through the door into her bedchamber.

Disappeared—Don Hedger was crouching on his knees, staring at the golden shower which poured in through the west windows, at the lake of gold sleeping on the faded Turkish carpet. The spot was enchanted; a vision out of Alexandria, out of the remote pagan past, had bathed itself there in Helianthine fire.

When he crawled out of his closet, he stood blinking at the grey sheet stuffed with laundry, not knowing what had

happened to him. He felt a little sick as he contemplated
the bundle. Everything here was different; he hated the disorder of the place, the grey prison light, his old shoes and
himself and all his slovenly habits. The black calico curtains
that ran on wires over his big window were white with
dust. There were three greasy frying pans in the sink, and
the sink itself—he felt desperate. He couldn't stand this
another minute. He took up an armful of winter clothes
and ran down four flights into the basement.

"Mrs. Foley," he began, "I want my room cleaned this
afternoon, thoroughly cleaned. Can you get a woman for
me right away?"

"Is it company you're having?" the fat, dirty janitress
enquired. Mrs. Foley was the widow of a useful Tammany
man, and she owned real estate in Flatbush. She was huge
and soft as a feather bed. Her face and arms were perma-
nently coated with dust, grained like wood where the sweat
had trickled.

"Yes, company. That's it."

"Well, this is a queer time of the day to be asking for a
cleaning woman. It's likely I can get you old Lizzie, if she's
not too drunk. I'll send Willy round to see."

Willy, the son of fourteen, roused from the stupor and
stain of his fifth box of cigarettes by the gleam of a quarter, went out. In five minutes he returned with old Lizzie—
she smelling strong of spirits and wearing several jackets
which she had put on one over the other, and a number of
skirts, long and short, which made her resemble an animated dish-clout. She had, of course, to borrow her equipment from Mrs. Foley, and toiled up the long flights,
dragging mop and pail and broom. She told Hedger to be

of good cheer, for he had got the right woman for the job, and showed him a great leather strap she wore about her wrist to prevent dislocation of tendons. She swished about the place, scattering dust and splashing soapsuds, while he watched her in nervous despair. He stood over Lizzie and made her scour the sink, directing her roughly, then paid her and got rid of her. Shutting the door on his failure, he hurried off with his dog to lose himself among the steve-dores and dock labourers on West Street.

A strange chapter began for Don Hedger. Day after day, at that hour in the afternoon, the hour before his neigh-bour dressed for dinner, he crouched down in his closet to watch her go through her mysterious exercises. It did not occur to him that his conduct was detestable; there was nothing shy or retreating about this unclad girl,—a bold body, studying itself quite coolly and evidently well pleased with itself, doing all this for a purpose. Hedger scarcely regarded his action as conduct at all; it was something that had happened to him. More than once he went out and tried to stay away for the whole afternoon, but at about five o'clock he was sure to find himself among his old shoes in the dark. The pull of that aperture was stronger than his will,—and he had always considered his will the strongest thing about him. When she threw herself upon the divan and lay resting, he still stared, holding his breath. His nerves were so on edge that a sudden noise made him start and brought out the sweat on his forehead. The dog would come and tug at his sleeve, knowing that something was wrong with his master. If he attempted a mournful whine, those strong hands closed about his throat.

When Hedger came slinking out of his closet, he sat

down on the edge of the couch, sat for hours without moving. He was not painting at all now. This thing, whatever it was, drank him up as ideas had sometimes done, and he sank into a stupor of idleness as deep and dark as the stupor of work. He could not understand it; he was no boy, he had worked from models for years, and a woman's body was no mystery to him. Yet now he did nothing but sit and think about one. He slept very little, and with the first light of morning he awoke as completely possessed by this woman as if he had been with her all the night before. The unconscious operations of life went on in him only to perpetuate this excitement. His brain held but one image now— vibrated, burned with it. It was a heathenish feeling; without friendliness, almost without tenderness.

Women had come and gone in Hedger's life. Not having had a mother to begin with, his relations with them, whether amorous or friendly, had been casual. He got on well with janitresses and wash-women, with Indians and with the peasant women of foreign countries. He had friends among the silk-skirt factory girls who came to eat their lunch in Washington Square, and he sometimes took a model for a day in the country. He felt an unreasoning antipathy toward the well-dressed women he saw coming out of big shops, or driving in the Park. If, on his way to the Art Museum, he noticed a pretty girl standing on the steps of one of the houses on upper Fifth Avenue, he frowned at her and went by with his shoulders hunched up as if he were cold. He had never known such girls, or heard them talk, or seen the inside of the houses in which they lived; but he believed them all to be artificial and, in an aesthetic sense, perverted. He saw them enslaved by desire of merchandise and manufactured articles, effective only in making life complicated and insincere and in embroidering it with ugly and meaningless trivialities. They were enough, he thought, to make one almost forget woman as she existed in art, in thought, and in the universe.

He had no desire to know the woman who had, for the time at least, so broken up his life,—no curiosity about her every-day personality. He shunned any revelation of it, and he listened for Miss Bower's coming and going, not to encounter, but to avoid her. He wished that the girl who wore shirt-waists and got letters from Chicago would keep out of his way, that she did not exist. With her he had naught to make. But in a room full of sun, before an old mirror, on a little enchanted rug of sleeping colours, he had seen a woman who emerged naked through a door, and disappeared naked. He thought of that body as never having been clad, or as having worn the stuffs and dyes of all the centuries but his own. And for him she had no geographical associations; unless with Crete, or Alexandria, or Veronese's Venice. She was the immortal conception, the perennial theme.

The first break in Hedger's lethargy occurred one afternoon when two young men came to take Eden Bower out to dine. They went into her music room, laughed and talked for a few minutes, and then took her away with them. They were gone a long while, but he did not go out for food himself; he waited for them to come back. At last he heard them coming down the hall, gayer and more talkative than when they left. One of them sat down at the piano, and they all began to sing. This Hedger found absolutely unendurable. He snatched up his hat and went running down the stairs. Caesar leaped beside him, hoping that old times were coming back. They had supper in the oysterman's basement and then sat down in front of their own doorway. The moon stood full over the Square, a thing of regal glory; but Hedger did not see the moon; he was looking, murderously, for men. Presently two, wearing straw hats and white trousers and carrying canes, came down the steps from his house. He rose and dogged them across the Square. They were laughing and seemed very much elated about something. As one stopped to light a cigarette, Hedger caught from the other:

"Don't you think she has a beautiful talent?"

His companion threw away his match. "She has a beautiful figure." They both ran to catch the stage.

Hedger went back to his studio. The light was shining from her transom. For the first time he violated her privacy at night, and peered through that fatal aperture. She was sitting, fully dressed, in the window, smoking a cigarette and looking out over the housetops. He watched her until she rose, looked about her with a disdainful, crafty smile, and turned out the light.

The next morning, when Miss Bower went out, Hedger followed her. Her white skirt gleamed ahead of him as she sauntered about the Square. She sat down behind the Garibaldi statue and opened a music book she carried. She turned the leaves carelessly, and several times glanced in his direction. He was on the point of going over to her, when she rose quickly and looked up at the sky. A flock of pigeons had risen from somewhere in the crowded Italian quarter to the south, and were wheeling rapidly up through the morning air, soaring and dropping, scattering and coming

together, now grey, now white as silver, as they caught or
intercepted the sunlight. She put up her hand to shade her
eyes and followed them with a kind of defiant delight in
her face.

Hedger came and stood beside her. "You've surely seen
them before?"

"Oh, yes," she replied, still looking up. "I see them every
day from my windows. They always come home about five
o'clock. Where do they live?"

"I don't know. Probably some Italian raises them for the
market. They were here long before I came, and I've been
here four years."

"In that gloomy room? Why didn't you take mine when
it was vacant?"

"It isn't gloomy. That's the best light for painting."

"Oh, is it? I don't know anything about painting. I'd like
to see your pictures sometime. You have such a lot in there.
Don't they get dusty, piled up against the wall like that?"

"Not very. I'd be glad to show them to you. Is your name
really Eden Bower? I've seen your letters on the table."

"Well, it's the name I'm going to sing under. My father's
name is Bowers, but my friend Mr. Jones, a Chicago newspaper man who writes about music, told me to drop the 's.'
He's crazy about my voice."

Miss Bower didn't usually tell the whole story,—about
anything. Her first name, when she lived in Huntington,
Illinois, was Edna, but Mr. Jones had persuaded her to change
it to one which he felt would be worthy of her future. She
was quick to take suggestions, though she told him she
"didn't see what was the matter with 'Edna.'"

She explained to Hedger that she was going to Paris to

study. She was waiting in New York for Chicago friends who were to take her over, but who had been detained. "Did you study in Paris?" she asked.

"No, I've never been in Paris. But I was in the south of France all last summer, studying with C——. He's the biggest man among the moderns,—at least I think so."

Miss Bower sat down and made room for him on the bench. "Do tell me about it. I expected to be there by this time, and I can't wait to find out what it's like."

Hedger began to relate how he had seen some of this Frenchman's work in an exhibition, and deciding at once that this was the man for him, he had taken a boat for Marseilles the next week, going over steerage. He proceeded at once to the little town on the coast where his painter lived, and presented himself. The man never took pupils, but because Hedger had come so far, he let him stay. Hedger lived at the master's house and every day they went out together to paint, sometimes on the blazing rocks down by the sea. They wrapped themselves in light woollen blankets and didn't feel the heat. Being there and working with C—— was being in Paradise, Hedger concluded; he learned more in three months than in all his life before.

Eden Bower laughed. "You're a funny fellow. Didn't you do anything but work? Are the women very beautiful? Did you have awfully good things to eat and drink?"

Hedger said some of the women were fine looking, especially one girl who went about selling fish and lobsters. About the food there was nothing remarkable,—except the ripe figs; he liked those. They drank sour wine, and used goat-butter, which was strong and full of hair, as it was churned in a goat skin.

"But don't they have parties or banquets? Aren't there any fine hotels down there?"

"Yes, but they are all closed in summer, and the country people are poor. It's a beautiful country, though."

"How, beautiful?" she persisted.

"If you want to go in, I'll show you some sketches, and you'll see."

Miss Bower rose. "All right. I won't go to my fencing lesson this morning. Do you fence? Here comes your dog. You can't move but he's after you. He always makes a face at me when I meet him in the hall, and shows his nasty little teeth as if he wanted to bite me."

In the studio Hedger got out his sketches, but to Miss Bower, whose favourite pictures were Christ Before Pilate and a redhaired Magdalen of Henner, these landscapes were not at all beautiful, and they gave her no idea of any country whatsoever. She was careful not to commit herself, however. Her vocal teacher had already convinced her that she had a great deal to learn about many things.

"Why don't we go out to lunch somewhere?" Hedger asked, and began to dust his fingers with a handkerchief—which he got out of sight as swiftly as possible.

"All right, the Brevoort," she said carelessly. "I think that's a good place, and they have good wine. I don't care for cocktails."

Hedger felt his chin uneasily. "I'm afraid I haven't shaved this morning. If you could wait for me in the Square? It won't take me ten minutes."

Left alone, he found a clean collar and handkerchief, brushed his coat and blacked his shoes, and last of all dug up ten dollars from the bottom of an old copper kettle he had brought from Spain. His winter hat was of such a complexion that the Brevoort hall boy winked at the porter as he took it and placed it on the rack in a row of fresh straw ones.

IV

That afternoon Eden Bower was lying on the couch in her music room, her face turned to the window, watching the pigeons. Reclining thus she could see none of the neighbouring roofs, only the sky itself and the birds that crossed and recrossed her field of vision, white as scraps of paper blowing in the wind. She was thinking that she was young and handsome and had had a good lunch, that a very easygoing, light-hearted city lay in the streets below her; and she was wondering why she found this queer painter chap, with his lean, bluish cheeks and heavy black eyebrows, more interesting than the smart young men she had met at her teacher's studio.

Eden Bower was, at twenty, very much the same person that we all know her to be at forty, except that she knew a great deal less. But one thing she knew: that she was to be Eden Bower. She was like some one standing before a great show window full of beautiful and costly things, deciding which she will order. She understands that they will arrive at her door. She already knew some of the many things that were to happen to her; for instance, that the Chicago millionaire who was going to take her abroad with his sister as chaperone, would eventually press his claim in quite another manner. He was the most circumspect of bachelors, afraid of everything obvious, even of women who were too flagrantly handsome. He was a nervous collector of pictures and furniture, a nervous patron of music, and a nervous host; very cautious about his health, and about any course of conduct that might make him ridiculous. But she knew that he would at last throw all his precautions to the winds.

People like Eden Bower are inexplicable. Her father sold farming machinery in Huntington, Illinois, and she had grown up with no acquaintances or experiences outside of that prairie town. Yet from her earliest childhood she had not one conviction or opinion in common with the people about her,—the only people she knew. Before she was out of short dresses she had made up her mind that she was going to be an actress, that she would live far away in great cities, that she would be much admired by men and would have everything she wanted. When she was thirteen, and was already singing and reciting for church entertainments, she read in some illustrated magazine a long article about the late Czar of Russia, then just come to the throne or about to come to it. After that, lying in the hammock on the front porch on summer evenings, or sitting through a long sermon in the family pew, she amused herself by trying to make up her mind whether she would or would not be the Czar's mistress when she played in his Capital. Now Edna had met this fascinating word only in the novels of Ouida,—her hard-worked little mother kept a long row of them in the upstairs storeroom, behind the linen chest. In Huntington, women who bore that relation to men were called by a very different name, and their lot was not an enviable one; of all the shabby and poor, they were the shabbiest. But then, Edna had never lived in Huntington, not even before she began to find books like "Sappho" and "Mademoiselle de Maupin," secretly sold in paper covers throughout Illinois. It was as if she had come into Huntington, into the Bowers family, on one of the trains that puffed over the marshes behind their back fence all day long, and was waiting for another train to take her out.

As she grew older and handsomer, she had many beaux, but these small-town boys didn't interest her. If a lad kissed her when he brought her home from a dance, she was indulgent and she rather liked it. But if he pressed her further, she slipped away from him, laughing. After she began to sing in Chicago, she was consistently discreet. She stayed as a guest in rich people's houses, and she knew that she was being watched like a rabbit in a laboratory. Covered up in bed, with the lights out, she thought her own thoughts, and laughed.

This summer in New York was her first taste of freedom. The Chicago capitalist, after all his arrangements were made for sailing, had been compelled to go to Mexico to look after oil interests. His sister knew an excellent singing master in New York. Why should not a discreet, well-balanced girl like Miss Bower spend the summer there, studying quietly? The capitalist suggested that his sister might enjoy a summer on Long Island; he would rent the Griffith's place for her, with all the servants, and Eden could stay there. But his sister met this proposal with a cold stare. So it fell out, that between selfishness and greed, Eden got a summer all her own,—which really did a great deal toward making her an artist and whatever else she was afterward to become. She had time to look about, to watch without being watched; to select diamonds in one window and furs in another, to select shoulders and moustaches in the big hotels where she went to lunch. She had the easy freedom of obscurity and the consciousness of power. She enjoyed both. She was in no hurry.

While Eden Bower watched the pigeons, Don Hedger sat on the other side of the bolted doors, looking into a pool of dark turpentine, at his idle brushes, wondering why a woman could do this to him. He, too, was sure of his future and knew that he was a chosen man. He could not know, of course, that he was merely the first to fall under a fascination which was to be disastrous to a few men and pleasantly stimulating to many thousands. Each of these two young people sensed the future, but not completely. Don Hedger knew that nothing much would ever happen to him. Eden Bower understood that to her a great deal would happen. But she did not guess that her neighbor would have more tempestuous adventures sitting in his dark studio than she would find in all the capitals of Europe, or in all the latitude of conduct she was prepared to permit herself.

V

One Sunday morning Eden was crossing the Square with a spruce young man in a white flannel suit and a panama hat. They had been breakfasting at the Brevoort and he was coaxing her to let him come up to her rooms and sing for an hour.

"No, I've got to write letters. You must run along now.

I see a friend of mine over there, and I want to ask him about something before I go up."

"That fellow with the dog? Where did you pick him up?" the young man glanced toward the seat under a sycamore where Hedger was reading the morning paper.

"Oh, he's an old friend from the West," said Eden easily. "I won't introduce you, because he doesn't like people. He's a recluse. Good-bye. I can't be sure about Tuesday. I'll go with you if I have time after my lesson." She nodded, left him, and went over to the seat littered with newspapers. The young man went up the Avenue without looking back.

"Well, what are you going to do today? Shampoo this animal all morning?" Eden enquired teasingly.

Hedger made room for her on the seat. "No, at twelve o'clock I'm going out to Coney Island. One of my models is going up in a balloon this afternoon. I've often promised to go and see her, and now I'm going."

Eden asked if models usually did such stunts. No, Hedger told her, but Molly Welch added to her earnings in that way. "I believe," he added, "she likes the excitement of it. She's got a good deal of spirit. That's why I like to paint her. So many models have flaccid bodies."

"And she hasn't, eh? Is she the one who comes to see you? I can't help hearing her, she talks so loud."

"Yes, she has a rough voice, but she's a fine girl. I don't suppose you'd be interested in going?"

"I don't know," Eden sat tracing patterns on the asphalt with the end of her parasol. "Is it any fun? I got up feeling I'd like to do something different today. It's the first Sunday I've not had to sing in church. I had that engagement for breakfast at the Brevoort, but it wasn't very exciting. That chap can't talk about anything but himself."

Hedger warmed a little. "If you've never been to Coney Island, you ought to go. It's nice to see all the people; tailors and bar-tenders and prize-fighters with their best girls, and all sorts of folks taking a holiday."

Eden looked sidewise at him. So one ought to be interested in people of that kind, ought one? He was certainly a funny fellow. Yet he was never, somehow, tiresome. She had seen a good deal of him lately, but she kept wanting to know him better, to find out what made him different from men like the one she had just left—whether he really was as different as he seemed. "I'll go with you," she said at last, "if you'll leave that at home." She pointed to Caesar's flickering ears with her sunshade.

"But he's half the fun. You'd like to hear him bark at the waves when they come in."

"No, I wouldn't. He's jealous and disagreeable if he sees you talking to any one else. Look at him now."

"Of course, if you make a face at him. He knows what that means, and he makes a worse face. He likes Molly Welch, and she'll be disappointed if I don't bring him."

Eden said decidedly that he couldn't take both of them. So at twelve o'clock when she and Hedger got on the boat at Desbrosses Street, Caesar was lying on his pallet, with a bone.

Eden enjoyed the boat-ride. It was the first time she had been on the water, and she felt as if she were embarking for France. The light warm breeze and the plunge of the waves made her very wide awake, and she liked crowds of any kind. They went to the balcony of a big, noisy restaurant and had a shore dinner, with tall steins of beer. Hedger had got a big advance from his advertising firm since he first lunched with Miss Bower ten days ago, and he was ready for anything.

After dinner they went to the tent behind the bathing beach, where the tops of two balloons bulged out over the canvas. A red-faced man in a linen suit stood in front of the tent, shouting in a hoarse voice and telling the people that if the crowd was good for five dollars more, a beautiful young woman would risk her life for their entertainment. Four little boys in dirty red uniforms ran about taking contributions in their pill-box hats. One of the balloons was bobbing up and down in its tether and people were shoving forward to get nearer the tent.

"Is it dangerous, as he pretends?" Eden asked.

"Molly says it's simple enough if nothing goes wrong with the balloon. Then it would be all over, I suppose."

"Wouldn't you like to go up with her?"

"I? Of course not. I'm not fond of taking foolish risks."

Eden sniffed. "I shouldn't think sensible risks would be very much fun."

Hedger did not answer, for just then every one began to shove the other way and shout, "Look out. There she goes!" and a band of six pieces commenced playing furiously.

As the balloon rose from its tent enclosure, they saw a girl in green tights standing in the basket, holding carelessly to one of the ropes with one hand and with the other waving to the spectators. A long rope trailed behind to keep the balloon from blowing out to sea.

As it soared, the figure in green tights in the basket diminished to a mere spot, and the balloon itself, in the brilliant light, looked like a big silver-grey bat, with its wings folded. When it began to sink, the girl stepped through the hole in the basket to a trapeze that hung below, and gracefully descended through the air, holding to the rod with both hands, keeping her body taut and her feet close together. The crowd, which had grown very large by this time, cheered vociferously. The men took off their hats and waved, little boys shouted, and fat old women, shining with the heat and a beer lunch, murmured admiring comments upon the balloonist's figure. "Beautiful legs, she has!"

"That's so," Hedger whispered. "Not many girls would look well in that position." Then, for some reason, he blushed a slow, dark, painful crimson.

The balloon descended slowly, a little way from the tent, and the red-faced man in the linen suit caught Molly Welch before her feet touched the ground, and pulled her to one side. The band struck up "Blue Bell" by way of welcome, and one of the sweaty pages ran forward and presented the balloonist with a large bouquet of artificial flowers. She smiled and thanked him, and ran back across the sand to the tent.

"Can't we go inside and see her?" Eden asked. "You can explain to the door man. I want to meet her." Edging forward, she herself addressed the man in the linen suit and slipped something from her purse into his hand.

They found Molly seated before a trunk that had a mirror in the lid and a "make-up" outfit spread upon the tray. She was wiping the cold cream and powder from her neck with a discarded chemise.

"Hello, Don," she said cordially. "Brought a friend?"

Eden liked her. She had an easy, friendly manner, and there was something boyish and devil-may-care about her.

"Yes, it's fun. I'm mad about it," she said in reply to Eden's questions. "I always want to let go, when I come down on the bar. You don't feel your weight at all, as you would on a stationary trapeze."

The big drum boomed outside, and the publicity man began shouting to newly arrived boatloads. Miss Welch took a last pull at her cigarette. "Now you'll have to get out, Don. I change for the next act. This time I go up in a black evening dress, and lose the skirt in the basket before I start down."

"Yes, go along," said Eden. "Wait for me outside the door. I'll stay and help her dress."

Hedger waited and waited, while women of every build bumped into him and begged his pardon, and the red pages ran about holding out their caps for coins, and the people ate and perspired and shifted parasols against the sun. When the band began to play a two-step, all the bathers ran up out of the surf to watch the ascent. The second balloon bumped and rose, and the crowd began shouting to the girl in a black evening dress who stood leaning against the ropes and smiling. "It's a new girl," they called. "It ain't the Countess this time. You're a peach, girlie!"

The balloonist acknowledged these compliments, bowing and looking down over the sea of upturned faces,—but Hedger was determined she should not see him, and he darted behind the tent-fly. He was suddenly dripping with cold sweat, his mouth was full of the bitter taste of anger and his tongue felt stiff behind his teeth. Molly Welch, in a shirt-waist and a white tam-o'-shanter cap, slipped out from the tent under his arm and laughed up in his face. "She's a crazy one you brought along. She'll get what she wants!"

"Oh, I'll settle with you, all right!" Hedger brought out with difficulty.

"It's not my fault, Donnie. I couldn't do anything with her. She bought me off. What's the matter with you? Are you soft on her? She's safe enough. It's as easy as rolling off a log, if you keep cool." Molly Welch was rather excited herself, and she was chewing gum at a high speed as she stood beside him, looking up at the floating silver cone. "Now watch," she exclaimed suddenly. "She's coming down on the bar. I advised her to cut that out, but you see she does it first-rate. And she got rid of the skirt, too. Those black tights show off her legs very well. She keeps her feet together like I told her, and makes a good line along the back. See the light on those silver slippers,—that was a good idea I had. Come along to meet her. Don't be a grouch; she's done it fine!"

Molly tweaked his elbow, and then left him standing like a stump, while she ran down the beach with the crowd.

Though Hedger was sulking, his eye could not help seeing the low blue welter of the sea, the arrested bathers, standing in the surf, their arms and legs stained red by the dropping sun, all shading their eyes and gazing upward at the slowly falling silver star.

Molly Welch and the manager caught Eden under the arms and lifted her aside, a red page dashed up with a bouquet, and the band struck up "Blue Bell." Eden laughed and bowed, took Molly's arm, and ran up the sand in her black tights and sliver slippers, dodging the friendly old women, and the gallant sports who wanted to offer their homage on the spot.

When she emerged from the tent, dressed in her own clothes, that part of the beach was almost deserted. She stepped to her companion's side and said carelessly: "Hadn't we better try to catch this boat? I hope you're not sore at me. Really, it was lots of fun."

Hedger looked at his watch. "Yes, we have fifteen minutes to get to the boat," he said politely.

As they walked toward the pier, one of the pages ran up panting. "Lady, you're carrying off the bouquet," he said, aggrievedly.

Eden stopped and looked at the bunch of spotty cotton roses in her hand. "Of course. I want them for a souvenir. You gave them to me yourself."

"I give 'em to you for looks, but you can't take 'em away. They belong to the show."

"Oh, you always use the same bunch?"

"Sure we do. There ain't too much money in this business."

She laughed and tossed them back to him. "Why are you angry?" she asked Hedger. "I wouldn't have done it if I'd been with some fellows, but I thought you were the sort who wouldn't mind. Molly didn't for a minute think you would."

"What possessed you to do such a fool thing?" he asked roughly.

"I don't know. When I saw her coming down, I wanted to try it. It looked exciting. Didn't I hold myself as well as she did?"

Hedger shrugged his shoulders, but in his heart he forgave her.

The return boat was not crowded, though the boats that passed them, going out, were packed to the rails. The sun was setting. Boys and girls sat on the long benches with their arms about each other, singing. Eden felt a strong wish to propitiate her companion, to be alone with him. She had been curiously wrought up by her balloon trip; it was a lark, but not very satisfying unless one came back to something after the flight. She wanted to be admired and adored. Though Eden said nothing, and sat with her arms limp on the rail in front of her, looking languidly at the rising silhouette of the city and the bright path of the sun, Hedger felt a strange drawing near to her. If he but brushed her white skirt with his knee, there was an instant communication between them, such as there had never been before. They did not talk at all, but when they went over the gangplank she took his arm and kept her shoulder close to his. He felt as if they were enveloped in a highly charged atmosphere, an invisible network of subtle, almost painful sensibility. They had somehow taken hold of each other.

An hour later, they were dining in the back garden of a little French hotel on Ninth Street, long since passed away. It was cool and leafy there, and the mosquitoes were not very numerous. A party of South Americans at another table were drinking champagne, and Eden murmured that she thought she would like some, if it were not too expensive. "Perhaps it will make me think I am in the balloon again. That was a very nice feeling. You've forgiven me, haven't you?"

Hedger gave her a quick straight look from under his black eyebrows, and something went over her that was like a chill, except that it was warm and feathery. She drank most of the wine; her companion was indifferent to it. He was talking more to her tonight than he had ever done before. She asked him about a new picture she had seen in his room; a queer thing full of stiff, supplicating female figures. "It's Indian, isn't it?"

"Yes. I call it Rain Spirits, or maybe, Indian Rain. In the Southwest, where I've been a good deal, the Indian traditions make women have to do with the rain-fall. They were supposed to control it, somehow, and to be able to find springs, and make moisture come out of the earth. You see I'm trying to learn to paint what people think and feel; to get away from all that photographic stuff. When I look at you, I don't see what a camera would see, do I?"

"How can I tell?"

"Well, if I should paint you, I could make you understand what I see." For the second time that day Hedger crimsoned unexpectedly, and his eyes fell and steadily contemplated a dish of little radishes. "That particular picture I got from a story a Mexican priest told me; he said he found it in an old manuscript book in a monastery down there, written by some Spanish Missionary, who got his stories from the Aztecs. This one he called 'The Forty Lovers of the Queen,' and it was more or less about rain-making."

"Aren't you going to tell it to me?" Eden asked.

Hedger fumbled among the radishes. "I don't know if it's the proper kind of story to tell a girl."

She smiled; "Oh, forget about that! I've been balloon riding today. I like to hear you talk."

Her low voice was flattering. She had seemed like clay in his hands ever since they got on the boat to come home. He leaned back in his chair, forgot his food, and, looking at her intently, began to tell his story, the theme of which he somehow felt was dangerous tonight.

The tale began, he said, somewhere in Ancient Mexico, and concerned the daughter of a king. The birth of this Princess was preceded by unusual portents. Three times her mother dreamed that she was delivered of serpents, which betokened that the child she carried would have power with the rain gods. The serpent was the symbol of water. The Princess grew up dedicated to the gods, and wise men taught her the rain-making mysteries. She was with difficulty restrained from men and was guarded at all times, for it was the law of the Thunder that she be maiden until her marriage. In the years of her adolescence, rain was abundant with her people. The oldest man could not remember such fertility. When the Princess had counted eighteen summers, her father went to drive out a war party that harried his borders on the north and troubled his prosperity. The King destroyed the invaders and brought home many prisoners. Among the prisoners was a young chief, taller than any of his captors, of such strength and ferocity that the King's people came a day's journey to look at him. When the Princess beheld his great stature, and saw that his arms and breast were covered with the figures of wild animals, bitten into the skin and coloured, she begged his life from her father. She desired that he should practise his art upon her, and prick upon her skin the signs of Rain and Lightning and Thunder, and stain the wounds with herb-juices, as they were upon his own body. For many days, upon the roof of the King's house, the Princess submitted herself to the bone needle, and the women with her marvelled at her fortitude. But the Princess was without shame before the Captive, and it came about that he threw from him his needles and his stains, and fell upon the Princess to violate her honour; and her women ran down from the roof screaming, to call the guard which stood at the gateway of the King's house, and none stayed to protect their mistress. When the guard came, the Captive was thrown into bonds, and he was gelded, and his tongue was torn out, and he was given for a slave to the Rain Princess.

The country of the Aztecs to the east was tormented by thirst, and their king, hearing much of the rain-making arts of the Princess, sent an embassy to her father, with presents and an offer of marriage. So the Princess went from her father to be the Queen of the Aztecs, and she took with her the Captive, who served her in everything with entire fidelity and slept upon a mat before her door.

The King gave his bride a fortress on the outskirts of the city, whither she retired to entreat the rain gods. This fortress was called the Queen's House, and on the night of the new moon the Queen came to it from the palace. But when the moon waxed and grew toward the round, because the god of Thunder had had his will of her, then the Queen returned to the King. Drought abated in the country and rain fell abundantly by reason of the Queen's power with the stars.

When the Queen went to her own house she took with her no servant but the Captive, and he slept outside her door and brought her food after she had fasted. The Queen had a jewel of great value, a turquoise that had fallen from the sun, and had the image of the sun upon it. And when she desired a young man whom she had seen in the army or among the slaves, she sent the Captive to him with the jewel, for a sign that he should come to her secretly at the Queen's House upon business concerning the welfare of all. And some, after she had talked with them, she sent away with rewards; and some she took into her chamber and kept them by her for one night or two. Afterward she called the Captive and bade him conduct the youth by the secret way he had come, underneath the chambers of the fortress. But for the going away of the Queen's lovers the Captive took out the bar that was beneath a stone in the floor of the passage, and put in its stead a rush-reed, and the youth stepped upon it and fell through into a cavern that was the bed of an underground river, and whatever was thrown into it was not seen again. In this service nor in any other did the Captive fail the Queen.

But when the Queen sent for the Captain of the Archers, she detained him four days in her chamber, calling often for food and wine, and was greatly content with him. On the fourth day she went to the Captive outside her door and said: "Tomorrow take this man up by the sure way, by which the King comes, and let him live."

In the Queen's door were arrows, purple and white. When she desired the King to come to her publicly, with his guard, she sent him a white arrow; but when she sent the purple, he came secretly, and covered himself with his mantle to be hidden from the stone gods at the gate. On the fifth night that the Queen was with her lover, the Captive took a purple arrow to the King, and the King came secretly and found them together. He killed the Captain with his own hand, but the Queen he brought to public trial. The Captive, when he was put to the question, told on his fingers forty men that he had let through the underground passage into the river. The Captive and the Queen were put to death by fire, both on the same day, and afterward there was scarcity of rain.

Eden Bower sat shivering a little as she listened. Hedger was not trying to please her, she thought, but to antagonize and frighten her by his brutal story. She had often told herself that his lean, big-boned lower jaw was like his bulldog's, but tonight his face made Caesar's most savage and determined expression seem an affectation. Now she was looking at the man he really was. Nobody's eyes had ever defied her like this. They were searching her and seeing everything; all she had concealed from Livingston, and from the millionaire and his friends, and from the newspaper men. He was testing her, trying her out, and she was more ill at ease than she wished to show.

"That's quite a thrilling story," she said at last, rising and winding her scarf about her throat. "It must be getting late. Almost every one has gone."

They walked down the Avenue like people who have quarrelled, or who wish to get rid of each other. Hedger did not take her arm at the street crossings, and they did not linger in the Square. At her door he tried none of the old devices of the Livingston boys. He stood like a post, having forgotten to take off his hat, gave her a harsh, threatening glance, muttered "good night," and shut his own door noisily.

There was no question of sleep for Eden Bower. Her brain was working like a machine that would never stop. After she undressed, she tried to calm her nerves by smoking a cigarette, lying on the divan by the open window. But she grew wider and wider awake, combating the challenge that had flamed all evening in Hedger's eyes. The balloon had been one kind of excitement, the wine another; but the thing that had roused her, as a blow rouses a proud man, was the doubt, the contempt, the sneering hostility with which the painter had looked at her when he told his savage story. Crowds and balloons were all very well, she reflected, but woman's chief adventure is man. With a mind over active and a sense of life over strong, she wanted to walk across the roofs in the starlight, to sail over the sea and face at once a world of which she had never been afraid.

Hedger must be asleep; his dog had stopped sniffing under the double doors. Eden put on her wrapper and slippers and stole softly down the hall over the old carpet; one loose board creaked just as she reached the ladder. The trapdoor was open, as always on hot nights. When she stepped out on the roof she drew a long breath and walked across it, looking up at the sky. Her foot touched something soft; she heard a low growl, and on the instant Caesar's sharp little teeth caught her ankle and waited. His breath was like steam on her leg. Nobody had ever intruded upon his roof before, and he panted for the movement or the word that would let him spring his jaw. Instead, Hedger's hand seized his throat.

"Wait a minute. I'll settle with him," he said grimly. He dragged the dog toward the manhole and disappeared. When he came back, he found Eden standing over by the dark chimney, looking away in an offended attitude.

"I caned him unmercifully," he panted. "Of course you didn't hear anything; he never whines when I beat him. He didn't nip you, did he?"

"I don't know whether he broke the skin or not," she answered aggrievedly, still looking off into the west.

"If I were one of your friends in white pants, I'd strike a match to find whether you were hurt, though I know you are not, and then I'd see your ankle, wouldn't I?"

"I suppose so."

He shook his head and stood with his hands in the pockets of his old painting jacket. "I'm not up to such boy-tricks. If you want the place to yourself, I'll clear out. There are plenty of places where I can spend the night, what's left of it. But if you stay here and I stay here—" He shrugged his shoulders.

Eden did not stir, and she made no reply. Her head drooped slightly, as if she were considering. But the moment he put his arms about her they began to talk, both at once, as people do in an opera. The instant avowal brought out a flood of trivial admissions. Hedger confessed his crime, was reproached and forgiven, and now Eden knew what it was in his look that she found so disturbing of late.

Standing against the black chimney, with the sky behind and blue shadows before, they looked like one of Hedger's own paintings of that period; two figures, one white and one dark, and nothing whatever distinguishable about them but that they were male and female. The faces were lost, the contours blurred in shadow, but the figures were a man and a woman, and that was their whole concern and their mysterious beauty,—it was the rhythm in which they moved, at last, along the roof and down into the dark hole; he first, drawing her gently after him. She came down very slowly. The excitement and bravado and uncertainty of that long day and night seemed all at once to tell upon her. When his feet were on the carpet and he reached up to lift her down, she twined her arms about his neck as after a long separation, and turned her face to him, and her lips, with their perfume of youth and passion.

One Saturday afternoon Hedger was sitting in the window of Eden's music room. They had been watching the pigeons come wheeling over the roofs from their unknown feeding grounds.

"Why," said Eden suddenly, "don't we fix those big doors into your studio so they will open? Then, if I want you, I won't have to go through the hall. That illustrator is loafing about a good deal of late."

"I'll open them, if you wish. The bolt is on your side."

"Isn't there one on yours, too?"

"No. I believe a man lived there for years before I came in, and the nurse used to have these rooms herself. Naturally, the lock was on the lady's side."

Eden laughed and began to examine the bolt. "It's all stuck up with paint." Looking about, her eye lighted upon a bronze Buddha which was one of the nurse's treasures. Taking him by his head, she struck the bolt a blow with his squatting posteriors. The two doors creaked, sagged, and swung weakly inward a little way, as if they were too old for such escapades. Eden tossed the heavy idol into a stuffed chair. "That's better," she exclaimed exultantly. "So the bolts are always on the lady's side? What a lot society takes for granted!"

Hedger laughed, sprang up and caught her arms roughly. "Whoever takes you for granted—Did anybody, ever?"

"Everybody does. That's why I'm here. You are the only one who knows anything about me. Now I'll have to dress if we're going out for dinner."

He lingered, keeping his hold on her. "But I won't always be the only one, Eden Bower. I won't be the last."

"No, I suppose not," she said carelessly. "But what does that matter? You are the first."

As a long, despairing whine broke in the warm stillness, they drew apart. Caesar, lying on his bed in the dark corner, had lifted his head at this invasion of sunlight, and realized that the side of his room was broken open, and his whole world shattered by change. There stood his master and this woman, laughing at him! The woman was pulling the long black hair of this mightiest of men, who bowed his head and permitted it.

VI

In time they quarrelled, of course, and about an abstraction,—as young people often do, as mature people almost never do. Eden came in late one afternoon. She had been with some of her musical friends to lunch at Burton Ives' studio, and she began telling Hedger about its splendours. He listened a moment and then threw down his brushes. "I know exactly what it's like," he said impatiently. "A very good department-store conception of a studio. It's one of the show places."

"Well, it's gorgeous, and he said I could bring you to see him. The boys tell me he's awfully kind about giving people a lift, and you might get something out of it."

Hedger started up and pushed his canvas out of the way. "What could I possibly get from Burton Ives? He's almost the worst painter in the world; the stupidest, I mean."

Eden was annoyed. Burton Ives had been very nice to her and had begged her to sit for him. "You must admit that he's a very successful one," she said coldly.

"Of course he is! Anybody can be successful who will do that sort of thing. I wouldn't paint his pictures for all the money in New York."

"Well, I saw a lot of them, and I think they are beautiful."

Hedger bowed stiffly.

"What's the use of being a great painter if nobody knows about you?" Eden went on persuasively. "Why don't you paint the kind of pictures people can understand, and then, after you're successful, do whatever you like?"

"As I look at it," said Hedger brusquely, "I am successful."

Eden glanced about. "Well, I don't see any evidences of it," she said, biting her lip. "He has a Japanese servant and a wine cellar, and keeps a riding horse."

Hedger melted a little. "My dear, I have the most expensive luxury in the world, and I am much more extravagant than Burton Ives, for I work to please nobody but myself."

"You mean you could make money and don't? That you don't try to get a public?"

"Exactly. A public only wants what has been done over and over. I'm painting for painters,—who haven't been born."

"What would you do if I brought Mr. Ives down here to see your things?"

"Well, for God's sake, don't! Before he left I'd probably tell him what I thought of him."

Eden rose. "I give you up. You know very well there's only one kind of success that's real."

"Yes, but it's not the kind you mean. So you've been thinking me a scrub painter, who needs a helping hand from some fashionable studio man? What the devil have you had anything to do with me for, then?"

"There's no use talking to you," said Eden, walking slowly toward the door. "I've been trying to pull wires for you all afternoon, and this is what it comes to." She had expected that the tidings of a prospective call from the great man would be received very differently, and had been thinking as she came home in the stage how, as with a magic wand, she might gild Hedger's future, float him out of his dark hole on a tide of prosperity, see his name in the papers and his pictures in the windows of Fifth Avenue.

Hedger mechanically snapped the midsummer leash on Caesar's collar and they ran downstairs and hurried through Sullivan Street off toward the river. He wanted to be among rough, honest people, to get down where the big drays bumped over stone paving blocks and the men wore corduroy trowsers and kept their shirts open at the neck. He stopped for a drink in one of the sagging bar-rooms on the water front. He had never in his life been so deeply wounded; he did not know he could be so hurt. He had told this girl all his secrets. On the roof, in these warm, heavy summer nights, with her hands locked in his, he had been able to explain all his misty ideas about an unborn art the world was waiting for; had been able to explain them better than he had ever done to himself. And she had looked away to the chattels of this uptown studio and coveted them for him! To her he was only an unsuccessful Burton Ives.

Then why, as he had put it to her, did she take up with him? Young, beautiful, talented as she was, why had she wasted herself on a scrub? Pity? Hardly; she wasn't sentimental. There was no explaining her. But in this passion that had seemed so fearless and so fated to be, his own position now looked to him ridiculous; a poor dauber without money or fame,—it was her caprice to load him with favours. Hedger ground his teeth so loud that his dog, trotting beside him, heard him and looked up.

While they were having supper at the oysterman's, he planned his escape. Whenever he saw her again, everything he had told her, that he should never have told any one, would come back to him; ideas he had never whispered even to the painter whom he worshipped and had gone all the way to France to see. To her they must seem his apology for not having horses and a valet, or merely the puerile boastfulness of a weak man. Yet if she slipped the bolt tonight and came through the doors and said, "Oh, weak man, I belong to you!" what could he do? That was the danger. He would catch the train out to Long Beach tonight, and tomorrow he would go on to the north end of Long Island, where an old friend of his had a summer studio among the sand dunes. He would stay until things came right in his mind. And she could find a smart painter, or take her punishment.

When he went home, Eden's room was dark; she was dining out somewhere. He threw his things into a hold-all he had carried about the world with him, strapped up some colours and canvases, and ran downstairs.

VII

Five days later Hedger was a restless passenger on a dirty, crowded Sunday train, coming back to town. Of course, he saw now how unreasonable he had been in expecting a Huntington girl to know anything about pictures; here was a whole continent full of people who knew nothing about pictures and he didn't hold it against them. What had such things to do with him and Eden Bower? When he lay out on the dunes, watching the moon come up out of the sea, it had seemed to him that there was no wonder in the world like the wonder of Eden Bower. He was going back to her because she was older than art, because she was the most overwhelming thing that had ever come into his life.

He had written her yesterday, begging her to be at home this evening, telling her that he was contrite, and wretched enough.

Now that he was on his way to her, his stronger feeling unaccountably changed to a mood that was playful and tender. He wanted to share everything with her, even the most trivial things. He wanted to tell her about the people on the train, coming back tired from their holiday with bunches of wilted flowers and dirty daisies; to tell her that the fish-man, to whom she had often sent him for lobsters, was among the passengers, disguised in a silk shirt and a spotted tie, and how his wife looked exactly like a fish, even to her eyes, on which cataracts were forming. He could tell her, too, that he hadn't as much as unstrapped his canvases,—that ought to convince her.

In those days passengers from Long Island came into New York by ferry. Hedger had to be quick about getting his dog out of the express car in order to catch the first boat. The East River, and the bridges, and the city to the west, were burning in the conflagration of the sunset; there was that great home-coming reach of evening in the air.

The car changes from Thirty-fourth Street were too many and too perplexing; for the first time in his life Hedger took a hansom cab for Washington Square. Caesar sat bolt upright on the worn leather cushion beside him, and they jogged off, looking down on the rest of the world.

It was twilight when they drove down lower Fifth Avenue into the Square, and through the Arch behind them were the two long rows of pale violet lights that used to bloom so beautifully against the grey stone and asphalt. Here and yonder about the Square hung globes that shed a radiance not unlike the blue mists of evening, emerging softly when daylight died, as the stars emerged in the thin blue sky. Under them the sharp shadows of the trees fell on the cracked pavement and the sleeping grass. The first stars and the first lights were growing silver against the gradual darkening, when Hedger paid his driver and went into the house,— which, thank God, was still there! On the hall table lay his letter of yesterday, unopened.

He went upstairs with every sort of fear and every sort of hope clutching at his heart; it was as if tigers were tearing him. Why was there no gas burning in the top hall? He found matches and the gas bracket. He knocked, but got no answer; nobody was there. Before his own door were exactly five bottles of milk, standing in a row. The milk-boy had taken spiteful pleasure in thus reminding him that he forgot to stop his order.

Hedger went down to the basement; it, too, was dark. The janitress was taking her evening airing on the basement steps. She sat waving a palm-leaf majestically, her dirty calico dress open at the neck. She told him at once that there had been "changes." Miss Bower's room was to let again, and the piano would go tomorrow. Yes, she left yesterday, she sailed for Europe with friends from Chicago. They arrived on Friday, heralded by many telegrams. Very rich people they were said to be, though the man had refused to pay the nurse a month's rent in lieu of notice,— which would have been only right, as the young lady had agreed to take the rooms until October. Mrs. Foley had observed, too, that he didn't overpay her or Willy for their trouble, and a great deal of trouble they had been put to, certainly. Yes, the young lady was very pleasant, but the nurse said there were rings on the mahogany table where she had put tumblers and wine glasses. It was just as well she was gone. The Chicago man was uppish in his ways, but not much to look at. She supposed he had poor health, for there was nothing to him inside his clothes.

Hedger went slowly up the stairs—never had they seemed so long, or his legs so heavy. The upper floor was emptiness and silence. He unlocked his room, lit the gas, and opened the windows. When he went to put his coat in the closet, he found, hanging among his clothes, a pale, flesh-tinted dressing gown he had liked to see her wear, with a per-fume—oh, a perfume that was still Eden Bower! He shut the door behind him and there, in the dark, for a moment he lost his manliness. It was when he held the garment to him that he found a letter in the pocket.

The note was written with a lead pencil, in haste: She was sorry that he was angry, but she still didn't know just what she had done. She had thought Mr. Ives would be useful to him; she guessed he was too proud. She wanted awfully to see him again, but Fate came knocking at her door after he had left her. She believed in Fate. She would never forget him, and she knew he would become the greatest painter in the world. Now she must pack. She hoped he wouldn't mind her leaving the dressing gown; somehow, she could never wear it again.

After Hedger read this, standing under the gas, he went back into the closet and knelt down before the wall; the knot hole had been plugged up with a ball of wet paper,— the same blue note-paper on which her letter was written.

He was hard hit. Tonight he had to bear the loneliness of a whole lifetime. Knowing himself so well, he could hardly believe that such a thing had happened to him, that such a woman had lain happy and contented in his arms. And now it was over. He turned out the light and sat down on his painter's stool before the big window. Caesar, on the floor beside him, rested his head on his master's knee. We must leave Hedger thus, sitting in his tank with his dog, looking up at the stars.

COMING, APHRODITE! This legend, in electric lights over the Lexington Opera House, had long announced the return of Eden Bower to New York after years of spectacular success in Paris. She came at last, under the management of an American Opera Company, but bringing her own *chef d'orchestre.*

One bright December afternoon Eden Bower was going down Fifth Avenue in her car, on the way to her broker, in Williams Street. Her thoughts were entirely upon stocks,—Cerro de Pasco, and how much she should buy of it,—when she suddenly looked up and realized that she was skirting Washington Square. She had not seen the place since she rolled out of it in an old-fashioned four-wheeler to seek her fortune, eighteen years ago.

"*Arrêtez, Alphonse. Attendez moi,*" she called, and opened the door before he could reach it. The children who were streaking over the asphalt on roller skates saw a lady in a long fur coat, and short, high-heeled shoes, alight from a French car and pace slowly about the Square, holding her muff to her chin. This spot, at least, had changed very little, she reflected; the same trees, the same fountain, the white arch, and over yonder, Garibaldi, drawing the sword for freedom. There, just opposite her, was the old red brick house.

"Yes, that is the place," she was thinking. "I can smell the carpets now, and the dog,—what was his name? That grubby bathroom at the end of the hall, and that dreadful Hedger— still, there was something about him, you know—" She glanced up and blinked against the sun. From somewhere in the crowded quarter south of the Square a flock of pigeons rose, wheeling quickly upward into the brilliant blue sky. She threw back her head, pressed her muff closer to her chin, and watched them with a smile of amazement and delight. So they still rose, out of all that dirt and noise and squalor, fleet and silvery, just as they used to rise that summer when she was twenty and went up in a balloon on Coney Island!

Alphonse opened the door and tucked her robes about her. All the way down town her mind wandered from Cerro de Pasco, and she kept smiling and looking up at the sky.

When she had finished her business with the broker, she asked him to look in the telephone book for the address of M. Gaston Jules, the picture dealer, and slipped the paper on which he wrote it into her glove. It was five o'clock when she reached the French Galleries, as they were called. On entering she gave the attendant her card, asking him to take it to M. Jules. The dealer appeared very promptly and begged her to come into his private office, where he pushed a great chair toward his desk for her and signalled his secretary to leave the room.

"How good your lighting is in here," she observed, glancing about. "I met you at Simon's studio, didn't I? Oh, no! I never forget anybody who interests me." She threw her muff on his writing table and sank into the deep chair. "I have come to you for some information that's not in my line. Do you know anything about an American painter named Hedger?"

He took the seat opposite her. "Don Hedger? But, certainly! There are some very interesting things of his in an exhibition at V——'s. If you would care to—"

She held up her hand. "No, no. I've no time to go to exhibitions. Is he a man of any importance?"

"Certainly. He is one of the first men among the moderns. That is to say, among the very moderns. He is always coming up with something different. He often exhibits in Paris, you must have seen—"

"No, I tell you I don't go to exhibitions. Has he had great success? That is what I want to know."

M. Jules pulled at his short grey moustache. "But, Madame, there are many kinds of success," he began cautiously.

Madame gave a dry laugh. "Yes, so he used to say. We once quarrelled on that issue. And how would you define his particular kind?"

M. Jules grew thoughtful. "He is a great name with all the young men, and he is decidedly an influence in art. But one can't definitely place a man who is original, erratic, and who is changing all the time."

She cut him short. "Is he much talked about at home? In Paris, I mean? Thanks. That's all I want to know." She rose and began buttoning her coat. "One doesn't like to have been an utter fool, even at twenty."

"Mais, non!" M. Jules handed her her muff with a quick,

sympathetic glance. He followed her out through the carpeted showroom, now closed to the public and draped in cheesecloth, and put her into her car with words appreciative of the honour she had done him in calling.

Leaning back in the cushions, Eden Bower closed her eyes, and her face, as the street lamps flashed their ugly orange light upon it, became hard and settled, like a plaster cast; so a sail, that has been filled by a strong breeze, behaves when the wind suddenly dies. Tomorrow night the wind would blow again, and this mask would be the golden face of Aphrodite. But a "big" career takes its toll, even with the best of luck.

A GOLD SLIPPER

Marshall McKann followed his wife and her friend Mrs. Post down the aisle and up the steps to the stage of the Carnegie Music Hall with an ill-concealed feeling of grievance. Heaven knew he never went to concerts, and to be mounted upon the stage in this fashion, as if he were a "highbrow" from Sewickley, or some unfortunate with a musical wife, was ludicrous. A man went to concerts when he was courting, while he was a junior partner. When he became a person of substance he stopped that sort of nonsense. His wife, too, was a sensible person, the daughter of an old Pittsburgh family as solid and well-rooted as the McKanns. She would never have bothered him about this concert had not the meddlesome Mrs. Post arrived to pay her a visit. Mrs. Post was an old school friend of Mrs. McKann, and because she lived in Cincinnati she was always keeping up with the world and talking about things in which no one else was interested, music among them. She was an aggressive lady, with weighty opinions, and a deep voice like a jovial bassoon. She had arrived only last night, and at dinner she brought it out that she could on no account miss Kitty Ayrshire's recital; it was, she said, the sort of thing no one could afford to miss.

When McKann went into town in the morning he found that every seat in the music-hall was sold. He telephoned his wife to that effect, and, thinking he had settled the matter, made his reservation on the 11.25 train for New York. He was unable to get a drawing-room because this same Kitty Ayrshire had taken the last one. He had not intended going to New York until the following week, but he preferred to be absent during Mrs. Post's incumbency.

In the middle of the morning, when he was deep in his correspondence, his wife called him up to say the enterprising Mrs. Post had telephoned some musical friends in Sewickley and had found that two hundred folding-chairs were to be placed on the stage of the concert-hall, behind the piano, and that they would be on sale at noon. Would he please get seats in the front row? McKann asked if they would not excuse him, since he was going over to New York on the late train, would be tired, and would not have time to dress, etc. No, not at all. It would be foolish for two women to trail up to the stage unattended. Mrs. Post's husband always accompanied her to concerts, and she expected that much attention from her host. He needn't dress, and he could take a taxi from the concert-hall to the East Liberty station.

The outcome of it all was that, though his bag was at the station, here was McKann, in the worst possible humour, facing the large audience to which he was well known, and sitting among a lot of music students and excitable old maids. Only the desperately zealous or the morbidly curious would endure two hours in those wooden chairs, and he sat in the front row of this hectic body, somehow made a party to a transaction for which he had the utmost contempt.

When McKann had been in Paris, Kitty Ayrshire was singing at the Comique, and he wouldn't go to hear her— even there, where one found so little that was better to do. She was too much talked about, too much advertised; always being thrust in an American's face as if she were something to be proud of. Perfumes and petticoats and cutlets were named for her. Some one had pointed Kitty out to him one afternoon when she was driving in the Bois with a French composer—old enough, he judged, to be her father—who was said to be infatuated, carried away by her. McKann was told that this was one of the historic passions of old age. He had looked at her on that occasion, but she was so befrilled and befeathered that he caught nothing but a graceful outline and a small, dark head above a white ostrich boa. He had noted with disgust, however, the stooped shoulders and white imperial of the silk-hatted man beside her, and the senescent line of his back. McKann described to his wife this unpleasing picture only last night, while he was undressing, when he was making every possible effort to avert this concert party. But Bessie only looked superior and said she wished to hear Kitty Ayrshire sing, and that her "private life" was something in which she had no interest.

Well, here he was; hot and uncomfortable, in a chair much too small for him, with a row of blinding footlights glaring in his eyes. Suddenly the door at his right elbow opened. Their seats were at one end of the front row; he had thought they would be less conspicuous there than in the centre, and he had not foreseen that the singer would walk over him every time she came upon the stage. Her velvet train brushed against his trousers as she passed him. The applause which greeted her was neither overwhelming nor prolonged. Her conservative audience did not know exactly how to accept her toilette. They were accustomed to dignified concert gowns, like those which Pittsburgh matrons (in those days!) wore at their daughters' coming-out teas.

Kitty's gown that evening was really quite outrageous—the repartée of a conscienceless Parisian designer who took her hint that she wished something that would be entirely novel in the States. Today, after we have all of us, even in the uttermost provinces, been educated by Bakst and the various Ballets Russes, we would accept such a gown without distrust; but then it was a little disconcerting, even to the well-disposed. It was constructed of a yard or two of green velvet—a reviling, shrieking green which would have made a fright of any woman who had not inextinguishable beauty—and it was made without armholes, a device to which we were then so unaccustomed that it was nothing less than alarming. The velvet skirt split back from a transparent gold-lace petticoat, gold stockings, gold slippers. The narrow train was, apparently, looped to both ankles, and it kept curling about her feet like a serpent's tail, turning up its gold lining as if it were squirming over on its back. It was not, we felt, a costume in which to sing Mozart and Handel and Beethoven.

Kitty sensed the chill in the air, and it amused her. She liked to be thought a brilliant artist by other artists, but by the world at large she liked to be thought a daring creature. She had every reason to believe, from experience and from example, that to shock the great crowd was the surest way to get its money and to make her name a household word. Nobody ever became a household word of being an artist, surely; and you were not a thoroughly paying proposition until your name meant something on the sidewalk and in the barbershop. Kitty studied her audience with an appraising eye. She liked the stimulus of this disapprobation. As she faced this hard-shelled public she felt keen and interested; she knew that she would give such a recital as cannot often be heard for money. She nodded gaily to the young man at the piano, fell into an attitude of seriousness, and began the group of Beethoven and Mozart songs.

Though McKann would not have admitted it, there were really a great many people in the concert-hall who knew what the prodigal daughter of their country was singing, and how well she was doing it. They thawed gradually under the beauty of her voice and the subtlety of her interpretation. She had sung seldom in concert then, and they had supposed her very dependent upon the accessories of the opera. Clean singing, finished artistry, were not what they expected from her. They began to feel, even, the wayward charm of her personality.

McKann, who stared coldly up at the balconies during her first song, during the second glanced cautiously at the green apparition before him. He was vexed with her for having retained a débutante figure. He comfortably classed all singers—especially operatic singers—as "fat Dutchwomen" or "shifty Sadies," and Kitty would not fit into his clever generalization. She displayed, under his nose, the only kind of figure he considered worth looking at—that of a very young girl, supple and sinuous and quick-silverish; thin, eager shoulders, polished white arms that were nowhere too fat and nowhere too thin. McKann found it agreeable to look at Kitty, but when he saw that the authoritative Mrs. Post, red as a turkey-cock with opinions she was bursting to impart, was studying and appraising the singer through her lorgnette, he gazed indifferently out into the house again. He felt for his watch, but his wife touched him warningly with her elbow—which, he noticed, was not at all like Kitty's.

When Miss Ayrshire finished her first group of songs, her audience expressed its approval positively, but guardedly. She smiled bewitchingly upon the people in front, glanced up at the balconies, and then turned to the company huddled on the stage behind her. After her gay and careless bows, she retreated toward the stage door. As she passed McKann, she again brushed lightly against him, and this time she paused long enough to glance down at him and murmur, "Pardon!"

In the moment her bright, curious eyes rested upon him, McKann seemed to see himself as if she were holding a mirror up before him. He beheld himself a heavy, solid figure, unsuitably clad for the time and place, with a florid, square face, well-visored with good living and sane opinions—an inexpressive countenance. Not a rock face, exactly, but a kind of pressed-brick-and-cement face, a "business" face upon which years and feelings had made no mark—in which cocktails might eventually blast out a few hollows. He had never seen himself so distinctly in his shaving-glass as he did in that instant when Kitty Ayrshire's liquid eye held him, when her bright, inquiring glance roamed over his person. After her prehensile train curled over his boot and she was gone, his wife turned to him and said in the tone of approbation one uses when an infant manifests its groping intelligence, "Very gracious of her, I'm sure!" Mrs. Post nodded oracularly. McKann grunted.

Kitty began her second number, a group of romantic German songs which were altogether more her affair than her first number. When she turned once to acknowledge the applause behind her, she caught McKann in the act of yawning behind his hand—he of course wore no gloves—and he thought she frowned a little. This did not embarrass him; it somehow made him feel important. When she retired after the second part of the program, she again looked him over curiously as she passed, and she took marked precaution that her dress did not touch him. Mrs. Post and his wife again commented upon her consideration.

The final number was made up of modern French songs which Kitty sang enchantingly, and at last her frigid public was thoroughly aroused. While she was coming back again and again to smile and curtsy, McKann whispered to his wife that if there were to be more encores he had better make a dash for his train.

"Not at all," put in Mrs. Post. "Kitty is going on the same train. She sings in *Faust* at the opera tomorrow night, so she'll take no chances."

McKann once more told himself how sorry he felt for Post. At last Miss Ayrshire returned, escorted by her accompanist, and gave the people what she of course knew they wanted: the most popular aria from the French opera of which the title-rôle had become synonymous with her name—an opera written for her and to her and round about her, by the veteran French composer who adored her,—the last and not the palest flash of his creative fire. This brought her audience all the way. They clamoured for more of it, but she was not to be coerced. She had been unyielding through storms to which this was a summer breeze. She came on once more, shrugged her shoulders, blew them a kiss, and was gone. Her last smile was for that uncomfortable part of her audience seated behind her, and she looked with recognition at McKann and his ladies as she nodded good night to the wooden chairs.

McKann hurried his charges into the foyer by the nearest exit and put them into his motor. Then he went over to the Schenley to have a glass of beer and a rarebit before train-time. He had not, he admitted to himself, been so much bored as he pretended. The minx herself was well enough, but it was absurd in his fellow-townsmen to look owlish and uplifted about her. He had no rooted dislike for pretty women; he even didn't deny that gay girls had their place in the world, but they ought to be kept in their place. He was born a Presbyterian, just as he was born a McKann. He sat in his pew in the First Church every Sunday, and he never missed a presbytery meeting when he was in town. His religion was not very spiritual, certainly, but it was substantial and concrete, made up of good, hard convictions and opinions. It had something to do with citizenship, with whom one ought to marry, with the coal business (in which his own name was powerful), with the Republican party, and with all majorities and established precedents. He was hostile to fads, to enthusiasms, to individualism, to all changes except in mining machinery and in methods of transportation.

His equanimity restored by his lunch at the Schenley, Mc-Kann lit a big cigar, got into his taxi, and bowled off through the sleet.

There was not a sound to be heard or a light to be seen. The ice glittered on the pavement and on the naked trees. No restless feet were abroad. At eleven o'clock the rows of small, comfortable houses looked as empty of the troublesome bubble of life as the Allegheny cemetery itself. Suddenly the cab stopped, and McKann thrust his head out of the window. A woman was standing in the middle of the street addressing his driver in a tone of excitement. Over against the curb a lone electric stood despondent in the storm. The young woman, her cloak blowing about her, turned from the driver to McKann himself, speaking rapidly and somewhat incoherently.

"Could you not be so kind as to help us? It is Mees Ayrshire, the singer. The juice is gone out and we cannot move. We must get to the station. Mademoiselle cannot miss the train; she sings tomorrow night in New York. It is very important. Could you not take us to the station at East Liberty?"

McKann opened the door. "That's all right, but you'll have to hurry. It's eleven-ten now. You've only got fifteen minutes to make the train. Tell her to come along."

The maid drew back and looked up at him in amazement. "But, the hand-luggage to carry, and Mademoiselle to walk! The street is like glass!"

McKann threw away his cigar and followed her. He

stood silent by the door of the derelict, while the maid explained that she had found help. The driver had gone off somewhere to telephone for a car. Miss Ayrshire seemed not at all apprehensive; she had not doubted that a rescuer would be forthcoming. She moved deliberately; out of a whirl of skirts she thrust one fur-topped shoe—McKann saw the flash of the gold stocking above it—and alighted.

"So kind of you! So fortunate for us!" she murmured. One hand she placed upon his sleeve, and in the other she carried an armful of roses that had been sent up to the concert stage. The petals showered upon the sooty, sleety pavement as she picked her way along. They would be lying there tomorrow morning, and the children in those houses would wonder if there had been a funeral. The maid followed with two leather bags. As soon as he had lifted Kitty into his cab she exclaimed:

"My jewel-case! I have forgotten it. It is on the back seat, please. I am so careless!"

He dashed back, ran his hand along the cushions, and discovered a small leather bag. When he returned he found the maid and the luggage bestowed on the front seat, and a place left for him on the back seat beside Kitty and her flowers.

"Shall we be taking you far out of your way?" she asked sweetly. "I haven't an idea where the station is. I'm not even sure about the name. Céline thinks it is East Liberty, but I think it is West Liberty. An odd name, anyway. It is a Bohemian quarter, perhaps? A district where the law relaxes a trifle?"

McKann replied grimly that he didn't think the name referred to that kind of liberty.

"So much the better," sighed Kitty. "I am a Californian; that's the only part of America I know very well, and out there, when we called a place Liberty Hill or Liberty Hollow—well, we meant it. You will excuse me if I'm uncommunicative, won't you? I must not talk in this raw air. My throat is sensitive after a long program." She lay back in her corner and closed her eyes.

When the cab rolled down the incline at East Liberty station, the New York express was whistling in. A porter opened the door. McKann sprang out, gave him a claim check and his Pullman ticket, and told him to get his bag at the check-stand and rush it on that train.

Miss Ayrshire, having gathered up her flowers, put out her hand to take his arm. "Why, it's you!" she exclaimed, as she saw his face in the light. "What a coincidence!" She made no further move to alight, but sat smiling as if she had just seated herself in a drawing-room and were ready for talk and a cup of tea.

McKann caught her arm. "You must hurry, Miss Ayrshire, if you mean to catch that train. It stops here only a moment. Can you run?"

"Can I run!" she laughed. "Try me!"

As they raced through the tunnel and up the inside stairway, McKann admitted that he had never before made a dash with feet so quick and sure stepping out beside him. The white-furred boots chased each other like lambs at play, the gold stockings flashed like the spokes of a bicycle wheel in the sun. They reached the door of Miss Ayrshire's state-room just as the train began to pull out. McKann was ashamed of the way he was panting, for Kitty's breathing was as soft and regular as when she was reclining on the back seat of his taxi. It was somehow run in his head that all these stage women were a poor lot physically—unsound, overfed creatures, like canaries that are kept in a cage and stuffed with song-restorer. He retreated to escape her thanks. "Good night! Pleasant journey! Pleasant dreams!" With a friendly nod in Kitty's direction he closed the door behind him.

He was somewhat surprised to find his own bag, his Pullman ticket in the strap, on the seat just outside Kitty's door. But there was nothing strange about it. He had got the last section left on the train, No. 13, next to the drawing-room. Every other berth in the car was made up. He was just starting to look for the porter when the door of the state-room opened and Kitty Ayrshire came out. She seated herself carelessly in the front seat beside his bag.

"Please talk to me a little," she said coaxingly. "I'm always wakeful after I sing, and I have to hunt some one to talk to. Céline and I get so tired of each other. We can speak very low, and we shall not disturb any one." She crossed her feet and rested her elbow on his Gladstone. Though she still wore her gold slippers and stockings, she did not, he thanked Heaven, have on her concert gown, but a very demure black velvet with some sort of pearl trimming about the neck. "Wasn't it funny," she proceeded, "that it happened to be you who picked me up? I wanted a word with you, anyway."

McKann smiled in a way that meant he wasn't being taken in. "Did you? We are not very old acquaintances."

"No, perhaps not. But you disapproved tonight, and I thought I was singing very well. You are very critical in such matters?"

He had been standing, but now he sat down. "My dear young lady, I am not critical at all. I know nothing about 'such matters.'"

"And care less?" she said for him. "Well, then we know where we are, in so far as that is concerned. What did displease you? My gown, perhaps? It may seem a little *outré* here, but it's the sort of thing all the imaginative designers abroad are doing. You like the English sort of concert gown better?"

"About gowns," said McKann, "I know even less than about music. If I looked uncomfortable, it was probably because I was uncomfortable. The seats were bad and the lights were annoying."

Kitty looked up with solicitude. "I was sorry they sold those seats. I don't like to make people uncomfortable in any way. Did the lights give you a headache? They are very trying. They burn one's eyes out in the end, I believe." She paused and waved the porter away with a smile as he came toward them. Half-clad Pittsburghers were tramping up and down the aisle, casting sidelong glances at McKann and his companion. "How much better they look with all their clothes on," she murmured. Then, turning directly to McKann again: "I saw you were not well seated, but I felt something quite hostile and personal. You were displeased with me. Doubtless many people are, but I seldom get an opportunity to question them. It would be nice if you took the trouble to tell me why you were displeased."

She spoke frankly, pleasantly, without a shadow of challenge or hauteur. She did not seem to be angling for compliments. McKann settled himself in his seat. He thought he would try her out. She had come for it, and he would

let her have it. He found, however, that it was harder to
formulate the grounds of his disapproval than he would
have supposed. Now that he sat face to face with her, now
that she was leaning against his bag, he had no wish to hurt
her.

"I'm a hard-headed business man," he said evasively,
"and I don't much believe in any of you fluffy-ruffles
people. I have a sort of natural distrust of them all, the men
more than the women."

She looked thoughtful. "Artists, you mean?" drawing
her words slowly. "What is your business?"

"Coal."

"I don't feel any natural distrust of business men, and I
know ever so many. I don't know any coal-men, but I think
I could become very much interested in coal. Am I larger-
minded than you?"

McKann laughed. "I don't think you know when you
are interested or when you are not. I don't believe you
know what it feels like to be really interested. There is so
much fake about your profession. It's an affectation on both
sides. I know a great many of the people who went to hear
you tonight, and I know that most of them neither know
nor care anything about music. They imagine they do,
because it's supposed to be the proper thing."

Kitty sat upright and looked interested. She was certainly a lovely creature—the only one of her tribe he had
ever seen that he would cross the street to see again. Those
were remarkable eyes she had—curious, penetrating, restless, somewhat impudent, but not at all dulled by self-
conceit.

"But isn't that so in everything?" she cried. "How many of your clerks are honest because of a fine, individual sense of honour? They are honest because it is the accepted rule of good conduct in business. Do you know"—she looked at him squarely—"I thought you would have something quite definite to say to me; but this is funny-paper stuff, the sort of objection I'd expect from your office-boy."

"Then you don't think it silly for a lot of people to get together and pretend to enjoy something they know nothing about?"

"Of course I think it silly, but that's the way God made audiences. Don't people go to church in exactly the same way? If there were a spiritual-pressure test-machine at the door, I suspect not many of you would get to your pews."

"How do you know I go to church?"

She shrugged her shoulders. "Oh, people with these old, ready-made opinions usually go to church. But you can't evade me like that." She tapped the edge of his seat with the toe of her gold slipper. "You sat there all evening, glaring at me as if you could eat me alive. Now I give you a chance to state your objections, and you merely criticize my audience. What is it? Is it merely that you happen to dislike my personality? In that case, of course, I won't press you."

"No," McKann frowned, "I perhaps dislike your professional personality. As I told you, I have a natural distrust of your variety."

"Natural, I wonder?" Kitty murmured. "I don't see why you should naturally dislike singers any more than I naturally dislike coal-men. I don't classify people by their occupations. Doubtless I should find some coal-men repulsive, and you may find some singers so. But I have reason to believe that, at least, I'm one of the less repellent."

"I don't doubt it," McKann laughed, "and you're a shrewd woman to boot. But you are, all of you, according to my standards, light people. You're brilliant, some of you, but you've no depth."

Kitty seemed to assent, with a dive of her girlish head. "Well, it's a merit in some things to be heavy, and in others to be light. Some things are meant to go deep, and others to go high. Do you want all the women in the world to be profound?"

"You are all," he went on steadily, watching her with indulgence, "fed on hectic emotions. You are pampered. You don't help to carry the burdens of the world. You are self-indulgent and appetent."

"Yes, I am," she assented, with a candor which he did not expect. "Not all artists are, but I am. Why not? If I could once get a convincing statement as to why I should not be self-indulgent, I might change my ways. As for the burdens of the world—" Kitty rested her chin on her clasped hands and looked thoughtful. "One should give pleasure to others. My dear sir, granting that the great majority of people can't enjoy anything very keenly, you'll admit that I give pleasure to many more people than you do. One should help others who are less fortunate; at present I am supporting just eight people, besides those I hire. There was never another family in California that had so many cripples and hard-luckers as that into which I had the honour to be born. The only ones who could take care of themselves were ruined by the San Francisco earthquake some time ago. One should make personal sacrifices. I do; I give money and time and effort to talented students. Oh, I give something much more than that! Something that you probably have never given to any one. I give, to the really gifted ones, my *wish,* my desire, my light, if I have any; and that, Mr. Worldly Wiseman, is like giving one's blood! It's the kind of thing you prudent people never give. That is what was in the box of precious ointment." Kitty drew off her fervour with a slight gesture, as if it were a scarf, and leaned back, tucking her slipper up on the edge of his seat. "If you saw the houses I keep up," she sighed, "and the people I employ, and the motor-cars I run—and, after all, I've only this to do it with." She indicated her slender person, which Marshall could almost have broken in two with his bare hands.

She was, he thought, very much like any other charming woman, except that she was more so. Her familiarity was natural and simple. She was at ease because she was not afraid of him or of herself, or of certain half-clad acquaintances of his who had been wandering up and down the car oftener than was necessary. Well, he was not afraid, either.

Kitty put her arms over her head and sighed again, feeling the smooth part in her black hair. Her head was small— capable of great agitation, like a bird's; or of great resignation, like a nun's. "I can't see why I shouldn't be self-indulgent, when I indulge others. I can't understand your equivocal scheme of ethics. Now I can understand Count Tolstoy's, perfectly. I had a long talk with him once, about his book 'What Is Art?' As nearly as I could get it, he believes that we are a race who can exist only by gratifying appetites;

the appetites are evil, and the existence they carry on is evil. We were always sad, he says, without knowing why; even in the Stone Age. In some miraculous way a divine ideal was disclosed to us, directly at variance with our appetites. It gave us a new craving, which we could only satisfy by starving all the other hungers in us. Happiness lies in ceasing to be and to cause being; because the thing revealed to us is dearer than any existence our appetites can ever get for us. I can understand that. It's something one often feels in art. It is even the subject of the greatest of all operas, which, because I can never hope to sing it, I love more than all the others." Kitty pulled herself up. "Perhaps you agree with Tolstoy?" she added languidly.

"No; I think he's a crank," said McKann, cheerfully.

"What do you mean by a crank?"

"I mean an extremist."

Kitty laughed. "Weighty word! You'll always have a world full of people who keep to the golden mean. Why bother yourself about me and Tolstoy?"

"I don't, except when you bother me."

"Poor man! It's true this isn't your fault. Still, you did provoke it by glaring at me. Why did you go to the concert?"

"I was dragged."

"I might have known!" she chuckled, and shook her head. "No, you don't give me any good reasons. Your morality seems to me the compromise of cowardice, apologetic and sneaking. When righteousness becomes alive and burning, you hate it as much as you do beauty. You want a little of each in your life, perhaps—adulterated, sterilized with the sting taken out. It's true enough they are both fearsome things when they get loose in the world; they don't, often."

McKann hated tall talk. "My views on women," he said slowly, "are simple."

"Doubtless," Kitty responded dryly, "but are they consistent? Do you apply them to your stenographers as well as to me? I take it for granted you have unmarried stenographers. Their position, economically, is the same as mine."

McKann studied the toe of her shoe. "With a woman, everything comes back to one thing." His manner was judicial.

She laughed indulgently. "So we are getting down to brass tacks, eh? I have beaten you in argument, and now you are leading trumps." She put her hands behind her head and her lips parted in a half-yawn. "Does everything come back to one thing? I wish I knew! It's more than likely that, under the same conditions, I should have been very like your stenographers—if they are good ones. Whatever I was, I would have been a good one. I think people are very much alike. You are more different than any one I have met for some time, but I know that there are a great many more at home like you. And even you—I believe there is a real creature down under these custom-made prejudices that save you the trouble of thinking. If you and I were shipwrecked on a desert island, I have no doubt that we would come to a simple and natural understanding. I'm neither a coward nor a shirk. You would find, if you had to undertake any enterprise of danger or difficulty with a woman, that there are several qualifications quite as important as the one to which you doubtless refer."

McKann felt nervously for his watch-chain. "Of course," he brought out, "I am not laying down any generalizations—" His brows wrinkled.

"Oh, aren't you?" murmured Kitty. "Then I totally misunderstood. But remember"—holding up a finger—"it is you, not I, who are afraid to pursue this subject further. Now, I'll tell you something." She leaned forward and clasped her slim, white hands about her velvet knee. "I am as much a victim of these ineradicable prejudices as you. Your stenographer seems to you a better sort. Well, she does to me. Just because her life is, presumably, greyer than mine, she seems better. My mind tells me that dullness, and a mediocre order of ability, and poverty, are not in themselves admirable things. Yet in my heart I always feel that the saleswomen in shops and the working girls in factories are more meritorious than I. Many of them, with my opportunities, would be more selfish than I am. Some of them, with their own opportunities, are more selfish. Yet I make this sentimental genuflection before the nun and the charwoman. Tell me, haven't you any weakness? Isn't there any foolish natural thing that unbends you a trifle and makes you feel gay?"

"I like to go fishing."

"To see how many fish you can catch?"

"No, I like the woods and the weather. I like to play a fish and work hard for him. I like the pussy-willows and the cold; and the sky, whether it's blue or grey—night coming on, every thing about it."

He spoke devoutly, and Kitty watched him through half-closed eyes. "And you like to feel that there are light-minded girls like me, who only care about the inside of shops and theatres and hotels, eh? You amuse me, you and your fish! But I mustn't keep you any longer. Haven't I given you every opportunity to state your case against me? I thought you would have more to say for yourself. Do you know, I believe it's not a case you have at all, but a grudge. I believe you are envious; that you'd like to be a tenor, and a perfect lady-killer!" She rose, smiling, and paused with her hand on the door of her state-room. "Anyhow, thank you for a pleasant evening. And, by the way, dream of me tonight, and not of either of those ladies who sat beside you. It does not matter much whom we live with in this world, but it matters a great deal whom we dream of." She noticed his bricky flush. "You are very naïf, after all, but, oh, so cautious! You are naturally afraid of everything new, just as I naturally want to try everything: new people, new religions—new miseries, even. If only there were more new things— If only you were really new! I might learn something. I'm like the Queen of Sheba—I'm not above learning. But you, my friend, would be afraid to try a new shaving soap. It isn't gravitation that holds the world in place; it's the lazy, obese cowardice of the people on it. All the same"—taking his hand and smiling encouragingly—"I'm going to haunt you a little. *Adios!*"

When Kitty entered her state-room, Céline, in her dressing-gown, was nodding by the window.

"Mademoiselle found the fat gentleman interesting?" she asked. "It is nearly one."

"Negatively interesting. His kind always say the same thing. If I could find one really intelligent man who held his views, I should adopt them."

"Monsieur did not look like an original," murmured Céline, as she began to take down her lady's hair.

McKann slept heavily, as usual, and the porter had to shake him in the morning. He sat up in his berth, and, after composing his hair with his fingers, began to hunt about for his clothes. As he put up the window-blind some bright object in the little hammock over his bed caught the sunlight and glittered. He stared and picked up a delicately turned gold slipper.

"Minx! Hussy!" he ejaculated. "All that tall talk—! Probably got it from some man who hangs about; learned it off like a parrot. Did she poke this in here herself last night, or did she send that sneak-faced Frenchwoman? I like her nerve!" He wondered whether he might have been breathing audibly when the intruder thrust her head between his curtains. He was conscious that he did not look a Prince Charming in his sleep. He dressed as fast as he could, and, when he was ready to go to the wash-room, glared at the slipper. If the porter should start to make up his berth in his absence— He caught the slipper, wrapped it in his pajama jacket, and thrust it into his bag. He escaped from the train without seeing his tormentor again.

Later McKann threw the slipper into the wastebasket in his room at the Knickerbocker, but the chambermaid, seeing that it was new and mateless, thought there must be a mistake, and placed it in his clothes-closet. He found it there when he returned from the theatre that evening. Considerably mellowed by food and drink and cheerful company, he took the slipper in his hand and decided to keep it as a reminder that absurd things could happen to people of the most clocklike deportment. When he got back to Pittsburgh, he stuck it in a lock-box in his vault, safe from prying clerks.

McKann has been ill for five years now, poor fellow! He still goes to the office, because it is the only place that interests him, but his partners do most of the work, and his clerks find him sadly changed—"morbid," they call his state of mind. He has had the pine-trees in his yard cut down because they remind him of cemeteries. On Sundays or holidays, when the office is empty, and he takes his will or his insurance-policies out of his lock-box, he often puts the tarnished gold slipper on his desk and looks at it. Somehow it suggests life to his tired mind, as his pine-trees suggested death—life and youth. When he drops over some day, his executors will be puzzled by the slipper.

As for Kitty Ayrshire, she has played so many jokes, practical and impractical, since then, that she has long ago forgotten the night when she threw away a slipper to be a thorn in the side of a just man.

A WAGNER MATINÉE

I received one morning a letter, written in pale ink on glassy, blue-lined note-paper, and bearing the postmark of a little Nebraska village. This communication, worn and rubbed, looking as if it had been carried for some days in a coat pocket that was none too clean, was from my uncle Howard, and informed me that his wife had been left a small legacy by a bachelor relative, and that it would be necessary for her to go to Boston to attend to the settling of the estate. He requested me to meet her at the station and render her whatever services might be necessary. On examining the date indicated as that of her arrival, I found it to be no later than tomorrow. He had characteristically delayed writing until, had I been away from home for a day, I must have missed my aunt altogether.

The name of my Aunt Georgiana opened before me a gulf of recollection so wide and deep that, as the letter dropped from my hand, I felt suddenly a stranger to all the present conditions of my existence, wholly ill at ease and out of place amid the familiar surroundings of my study. I became, in short, the gangling farmer-boy my aunt had known, scourged with chilblains and bashfulness, my hands cracked and sore from the corn husking. I sat again before her parlour organ, fumbling the scales with my stiff, red fingers, while she, beside me, made canvas mittens for the huskers.

The next morning, after preparing my landlady for a visitor, I set out for the station. When the train arrived I had some difficulty in finding my aunt. She was the last of the passengers to alight, and it was not until I got her into the carriage that she seemed really to recognize me. She had come all the way in a day coach; her linen duster had become black with soot and her black bonnet grey with dust during the journey. When we arrived at my boarding-house the landlady put her to bed at once and I did not see her again until the next morning.

Whatever shock Mrs. Springer experienced at my aunt's appearance, she considerately concealed. As for myself, I saw my aunt's battered figure with that feeling of awe and respect with which we behold explorers who have left their ears and fingers north of Franz-Joseph-Land, or their health somewhere along the Upper Congo. My Aunt Georgiana had been a music teacher at the Boston Conservatory, somewhere back in the latter sixties. One summer, while visiting in the little village among the Green Mountains where her ancestors had dwelt for generations, she had kindled the callow fancy of my uncle, Howard Carpenter, then an idle, shiftless boy of twenty-one. When she returned to her duties in Boston, Howard followed her, and the upshot of this infatuation was that she eloped with him, eluding the reproaches of her family and the criticism of her friends by going with him to the Nebraska frontier. Carpenter, who, of course, had no money, took up a homestead in Red Willow County, fifty miles from the railroad. There they had measured off their land themselves, driving across the prairie in a wagon, to the wheel of which they had tied a red cotton handkerchief, and counting its revolutions. They built a dug-out in the red hillside, one of those cave dwellings whose inmates so often reverted to primitive conditions. Their water they got from the lagoons where the buffalo drank, and their slender stock of provisions was always at the mercy of bands of roving Indians. For thirty years my aunt had not been farther than fifty miles from the homestead.

I owed to this woman most of the good that ever came my way in my boyhood, and had a reverential affection for her. During the years when I was riding herd for my uncle, my aunt, after cooking the three meals—the first of which was ready at six o'clock in the morning—and putting the six children to bed, would often stand until midnight at her ironing-board, with me at the kitchen table beside her, hearing me recite Latin declensions and conjugations, gently shaking me when my drowsy head sank down over a page of irregular verbs. It was to her, at her ironing or mending, that I read my first Shakespeare, and her old text-book on mythology was the first that ever came into my empty hands. She taught me my scales and exercises on the little parlour organ which her husband had bought her after fifteen years during which she had not so much as seen a musical instrument. She would sit beside me by the hour, darning and counting, while I struggled with the "Joyous Farmer." She seldom talked to me about music, and I understood why. Once when I had been doggedly beating out some easy passages from an old score of *Euryanthe* I had found among her music books, she came up to me and, putting her hands over my eyes, gently drew my head back upon her shoulder, saying tremulously, "Don't love it so well, Clark, or it may be taken from you."

When my aunt appeared on the morning after her arrival in Boston, she was still in a semi-somnambulant state. She seemed not to realize that she was in the city where she had spent her youth, the place longed for hungrily half a lifetime. She had been so wretchedly train-sick throughout the journey that she had no recollection of anything but her discomfort, and, to all intents and purposes, there were but a few hours of nightmare between the farm in Red Willow County and my study on Newbury Street. I had planned a little pleasure for her that afternoon, to repay her for some of the glorious moments she had given me when we used to milk together in the straw-thatched cowshed and she, because I was more than usually tired, or because her husband had spoken sharply to me, would tell me of the splendid performance of the *Huguenots* she had seen in Paris, in her youth.

At two o'clock the Symphony Orchestra was to give a Wagner program, and I intended to take my aunt; though, as I conversed with her, I grew doubtful about her enjoyment of it. I suggested our visiting the Conservatory and the Common before lunch, but she seemed altogether too timid to wish to venture out. She questioned me absently about various changes in the city, but she was chiefly concerned that she had forgotten to leave instructions about feeding half-skimmed milk to a certain weakling calf, "old

Maggie's calf, you know, Clark," she explained, evidently having forgotten how long I had been away. She was further troubled because she had neglected to tell her daughter about the freshly-opened kit of mackerel in the cellar, which would spoil if it were not used directly.

I asked her whether she had ever heard any of the Wagnerian operas, and found that she had not, though she was perfectly familiar with their respective situations, and had once possessed the piano score of *The Flying Dutchman*. I began to think it would be best to get her back to Red Willow County without waking her, and regretted having suggested the concert.

From the time we entered the concert hall, however, she was a trifle less passive and inert, and for the first time seemed to perceive her surroundings. I had felt some trepidation lest she might become aware of her queer, country clothes, or might experience some painful embarrassment at stepping suddenly into the world to which she had been dead for a quarter of a century. But, again, I found how superficially I had judged her. She sat looking about her with eyes as impersonal, almost as stony, as those with which the granite Rameses in a museum watches the froth and fret that ebbs and flows about his pedestal. I have seen this same aloofness in old miners who drift into the Brown hotel at Denver, their pockets full of bullion, their linen soiled, their haggard faces unshaven; standing in the thronged corridors as solitary as though they were still in a frozen camp on the Yukon.

The matinée audience was made up chiefly of women. One lost the contour of faces and figures, indeed any effect of the line whatever, and there was only the colour of bodices past counting, the shimmer of fabrics soft and firm, silky and sheer; red, mauve, pink, blue, lilac, purple, écru, rose, yellow, cream, and white, all the colours that an impressionist finds in a sunlit landscape, with here and there the dead shadow of a frock coat. My Aunt Georgiana regarded them as though they had been so many daubs of tube-paint on a palette.

When the musicians came out and took their places, she gave a little stir of anticipation, and looked with quickening interest down over the rail at that invariable grouping, perhaps the first wholly familiar thing that had greeted her eye since she had left old Maggie and her weakling calf. I could feel how all those details sank into her soul, for I had not forgotten how they had sunk into mine when I came fresh from ploughing forever and forever between green aisles of corn, where, as in a treadmill, one might walk from daybreak to dusk without perceiving a shadow of change. The clean profiles of the musicians, the gloss of their linen, the dull black of their coats, the beloved shapes of the instruments, the patches of yellow light on the smooth, varnished bellies of the 'cellos and the bass viols in the rear, the restless, wind-tossed forest of fiddle necks and bows—I recalled how, in the first orchestra I ever heard, those long bow-strokes seemed to draw the heart out of me, as a conjurer's stick reels out yards of paper ribbon from a hat.

The first number was the *Tannhäuser* overture. When the horns drew out the first strain of the Pilgrim's chorus, Aunt Georgiana clutched my coat sleeve. Then it was I first realized that for her this broke a silence of thirty years. With the battle between the two motives, with the frenzy of the Venusberg theme and its ripping of strings, there came to me an overwhelming sense of the waste and wear we are so powerless to combat; and I saw again the tall, naked house on the prairie, black and grim as a wooden fortress; the black pond where I had learned to swim, its margin pitted with sun-dried cattle tracks; the rain-gullied clay banks about the naked house, the four dwarf ash seedlings where the dish-cloths were always hung to dry before the kitchen door. The world there was the flat world of the ancients; to the east, a cornfield that stretched to daybreak; to the west, a corral that reached to sunset; between, the conquests of peace, dearer-bought than those of war.

The overture closed, my aunt released my coat sleeve, but she said nothing. She sat staring dully at the orchestra. What, I wondered, did she get from it? She had been a good pianist in her day, I knew, and her musical education had been broader than that of most music teachers a quarter of a century ago. She had often told me of Mozart's operas and Meyerbeer's, and I could remember hearing her sing, years ago, certain melodies of Verdi. When I had fallen ill with a fever in her house she used to sit by my cot in the evening—when the cool, night wind blew in through the faded mosquito netting tacked over the window and I lay watching a certain bright star that burned red above the cornfield—and sing "Home to our mountains, O, let us return!" in a way fit to break the heart of a Vermont boy near dead of home-sickness already.

I watched her closely through the prelude to *Tristan and Isolde,* trying vainly to conjecture what that seething turmoil of strings and winds might mean to her, but she sat

mutely staring at the violin bows that drove obliquely
downward, like the pelting streaks of rain in a summer
shower. Had this music any message for her? Had she
enough left to at all comprehend this power which had
kindled the world since she had left it? I was in a fever of
curiosity, but Aunt Georgiana sat silent upon her peak in
Darien. She preserved this utter immobility throughout
the number from *The Flying Dutchman,* though her fingers
worked mechanically upon her black dress, as if, of themselves, they were recalling the piano score they had once
played. Poor hands! They had been stretched and twisted
into mere tentacles to hold and lift and knead with;—on
one of them a thin, worn band that had once been a wedding ring. As I pressed and gently quieted one of those
groping hands, I remembered with quivering eyelids their
services for me in other days.

Soon after the tenor began the "Prize Song," I heard a
quick drawn breath and turned to my aunt. Her eyes were
closed, but the tears were glistening on her cheeks, and
I think, in a moment more, they were in my eyes as well.
It never really died, then—the soul which can suffer so
excruciatingly and so interminably; it withers to the outward eye only, like that strange moss which can lie on a
dusty shelf half a century and yet, if placed in water, grows
green again. She wept so throughout the development and
elaboration of the melody.

During the intermission before the second half, I questioned my aunt and found that the "Prize Song" was not
new to her. Some years before there had drifted to the
farm in Red Willow County a young German, a tramp
cow-puncher, who had sung in the chorus at Bayreuth

when he was a boy, along with the other peasant boys and girls. Of a Sunday morning he used to sit on his gingham-sheeted bed in the hands' bedroom which opened off the kitchen, cleaning the leather of his boots and saddle, singing the "Prize Song," while my aunt went about her work in the kitchen. She had hovered over him until she had prevailed upon him to join the country church, though his sole fitness for this step, in so far as I could gather, lay in his boyish face and his possession of this divine melody. Shortly afterward, he had gone to town on the Fourth of July, been drunk for several days, lost his money at a faro table, ridden a saddled Texas steer on a bet, and disappeared with a fractured collar-bone. All this my aunt told me huskily, wanderingly, as though she were talking in the weak lapses of illness.

"Well, we have come to better things than the old *Trovatore* at any rate, Aunt Georgie?" I queried, with a well-meant effort at jocularity.

Her lip quivered and she hastily put her handkerchief up to her mouth. From behind it she murmured, "And you have been hearing this ever since you left me, Clark?" Her question was the gentlest and saddest of reproaches.

The second half of the program consisted of four numbers from the *Ring,* and closed with Siegfried's funeral march. My aunt wept quietly, but almost continuously, as a shallow vessel overflows in a rain-storm. From time to time her dim eyes looked up at the lights, burning softly under their dull glass globes.

The deluge of sound poured on and on; I never knew what she found in the shining current of it; I never knew how far it bore her, or past what happy islands. From the trembling of her face I could well believe that before the last number she had been carried out where the myriad graves are, into the grey, nameless burying grounds of the sea; or into some world of death vaster yet, where, from the beginning of the world, hope has lain down with hope and dream with dream and, renouncing, slept.

The concert was over; the people filed out of the hall chattering and laughing, glad to relax and find the living level again, but my kinswoman made no effort to rise. The harpist slipped the green felt cover over his instrument; the flute-players shook the water from their mouth-pieces; the men of the orchestra went one by one, leaving the stage to the chairs and music stands, empty as a winter cornfield.

I spoke to my aunt. She burst into tears and sobbed pleadingly. "I don't want to go, Clark, I don't want to go!"

I understood. For her, just outside the concert hall, lay the black pond with the cattle-tracked bluffs; the tall, un-painted house, with weather-curled boards, naked as a tower; the crook-backed ash seedlings where the dish-cloths hung to dry; the gaunt, moulting turkeys picking up refuse about the kitchen door.

from ONE OF OURS

I

Claude Wheeler opened his eyes before the sun was up and vigorously shook his younger brother, who lay in the other half of the same bed.

"Ralph, Ralph, get awake! Come down and help me wash the car."

"What for?"

"Why, aren't we going to the circus today?"

"Car's all right. Let me alone." The boy turned over and pulled the sheet up to his face, to shut out the light which was beginning to come through the curtainless windows.

Claude rose and dressed,—a simple operation which took very little time. He crept down two flights of stairs, feeling his way in the dusk, his red hair standing up in peaks, like a cock's comb. He went through the kitchen into the adjoining washroom, which held two porcelain stands with running water. Everybody had washed before going to bed, apparently, and the bowls were ringed with a dark sediment which the hard, alkaline water had not dissolved. Shutting the door on this disorder, he turned back to the kitchen, took Mahailey's tin basin, doused his face and head in cold water, and began to plaster down his wet hair.

Old Mahailey herself came in from the yard, with her apron full of corn-cobs to start a fire in the kitchen stove. She smiled at him in the foolish fond way she often had with them when they were alone.

"What air you gittin' up for a-ready, boy? You goin' to the circus before breakfast? Don't make no noise, else you'll have 'em all down here before I git my fire a-goin'."

"All right, Mahailey." Claude caught up his cap and ran out of doors, down the hillside toward the barn. The sun popped up over the edge of the prairie like a broad, smiling face; the light poured across the close-cropped August pastures and the hilly, timbered windings of Lovely Creek,— a clear little stream with a sand bottom, that curled and twisted playfully about through the south section of the big Wheeler ranch. It was a fine day to go to the circus at Frankfort, a fine day to do anything; the sort of day that must, somehow, turn out well.

Claude backed the little Ford car out of its shed, ran it up to the horse-tank, and began to throw water on the mud crusted wheels and windshield. While he was at work the two hired men, Dan and Jerry, came shambling down the hill to feed the stock. Jerry was grumbling and swearing about something, but Claude wrung out his wet rags and, beyond a nod, paid no attention to them. Somehow his father always managed to have the roughest and dirtiest hired men in the country working for him. Claude had a grievance against Jerry just now, because of his treatment of one of the horses.

Molly was a faithful old mare, the mother of many colts; Claude and his younger brother had learned to ride on her. This man Jerry, taking her out to work one morning, let her step on a board with a nail sticking up in it. He pulled the nail out of her foot, said nothing to anybody, and drove her to the cultivator all day. Now she had been standing in her stall for weeks, patiently suffering, her body wretchedly thin, and her leg swollen until it looked like an elephant's. She would have to stand there, the veterinary said, until her hoof came off and she grew a new one, and she would always be stiff. Jerry had not been discharged, and he exhibited the poor animal as if she were a credit to him.

Mahailey came out on the hilltop and rang the breakfast bell. After the hired men went up to the house, Claude slipped into the barn to see that Molly had got her share of oats. She was eating quietly, her head hanging, and her scaly, dead-looking foot lifted just a little from the ground. When he stroked her neck and talked to her she stopped grinding and gazed at him mournfully. She knew him, and wrinkled her nose and drew her upper lip back from her worn teeth, to show that she liked being petted. She let him touch her foot and examine her legs.

When Claude reached the kitchen, his mother was sitting at one end of the breakfast table, pouring weak coffee, his brother and Danny and Jerry were in their chairs, and Mahailey was baking griddle cakes at the stove. A moment later Mr. Wheeler came down the enclosed stairway and walked the length of the table to his own place. He was a very large man, taller and broader than any of his neighbours. He seldom wore a coat in summer, and his rumpled shirt bulged out carelessly over the belt of his trousers. His florid face was clean shaven, likely to be a trifle tobacco-stained about the mouth, and it was conspicuous both for good-nature and coarse humour, and for an imperturbable physical composure. Nobody in the county had ever seen Nat Wheeler flustered about anything, and nobody had ever heard him speak with complete seriousness. He kept up his easy-going, jocular affability even with his own family.

As soon as he was seated, Mr. Wheeler reached for the two-pint sugar bowl and began to pour sugar into his coffee. Ralph asked him if he were going to the circus. Mr. Wheeler winked.

"I shouldn't wonder if I happened in town sometime before the elephants get away." He spoke very deliberately, with a State-of-Maine drawl, and his voice was smooth and agreeable. "You boys better start in early, though. You can take the wagon and the mules, and load in the cowhides. The butcher has agreed to take them."

Claude put down his knife. "Can't we have the car? I've washed it on purpose."

"And what about Dan and Jerry? They want to see the circus just as much as you do, and I want the hides should go in; they're bringing a good price now. I don't mind about your washing the car; mud preserves the paint, they say, but it'll be all right this time, Claude."

The hired men haw-hawed and Ralph giggled. Claude's freckled face got very red. The pancake grew stiff and heavy in his mouth and was hard to swallow. His father knew he hated to drive the mules to town, and knew how he hated to go anywhere with Dan and Jerry. As for the hides, they were the skins of four steers that had perished in the blizzard last winter through the wanton carelessness of these same hired men, and the price they would bring would not half pay for the time his father had spent in stripping and curing them. They had lain in a shed loft all summer, and the wagon had been to town a dozen times. But today, when he wanted to go to Frankfort clean and care-free, he must take these stinking hides and two coarse-mouthed men, and drive a pair of mules that always brayed and balked and behaved ridiculously in a crowd. Probably his father had looked out of the window and seen him washing the car, and had put this up on him while he dressed. It was like his father's idea of a joke.

Mrs. Wheeler looked at Claude sympathetically, feeling that he was disappointed. Perhaps she, too, suspected a joke. She had learned that humour might wear almost any guise.

When Claude started for the barn after breakfast, she came running down the path, calling to him faintly,— hurrying always made her short of breath. Overtaking him, she looked up with solicitude, shading her eyes with her delicately formed hand. "If you want I should do up your linen coat, Claude, I can iron it while you're hitching," she said wistfully.

Claude stood kicking at a bunch of mottled feathers that had once been a young chicken. His shoulders were drawn high, his mother saw, and his figure suggested energy and determined self-control.

"You needn't mind, mother." He spoke rapidly, muttering his words. "I'd better wear my old clothes if I have to take the hides. They're greasy, and in the sun they'll smell worse than fertilizer."

"The men can handle the hides, I should think. Wouldn't you feel better in town to be dressed?" She was still blinking up at him.

"Don't bother about it. Put me out a clean coloured shirt, if you want to. That's all right."

He turned toward the barn, and his mother went slowly back the path up to the house. She was so plucky and so stooped, his dear mother! He guessed if she could stand having these men about, could cook and wash for them, he could drive them to town!

Half an hour after the wagon left, Nat Wheeler put on an alpaca coat and went off in the rattling buckboard in which, though he kept two automobiles, he still drove about the country. He said nothing to his wife; it was her business to guess whether or not he would be home for dinner. She and Mahailey could have a good time scrubbing and sweeping all day, with no men around to bother them.

There were few days in the year when Wheeler did not drive off somewhere; to an auction sale, or a political convention, or a meeting of the Farmers' Telephone directors;—to see how his neighbours were getting on with their work, if there was nothing else to look after. He preferred his buckboard to a car because it was light, went easily over heavy or rough roads, and was so rickety that he never felt he must suggest his wife's accompanying him. Besides he could see the country better when he didn't have to keep his mind on the road. He had come to this part of Nebraska when the Indians and the buffalo were still about, remembered the grasshopper year and the big cyclone, had watched the farms emerge one by one from the great rolling page where once only the wind wrote its story. He had encouraged new settlers to take up home-steads, urged on courtships, lent young fellows the money to marry on, seen families grow and prosper; until he felt a little as if all this were his own enterprise. The changes, not only those the years made, but those the seasons made, were interesting to him.

People recognized Nat Wheeler and his car a mile away. He sat massive and comfortable, weighing down one end of the slanting seat, his driving hand lying on his knee. Even his German neighbours, the Yoeders, who hated to stop work for a quarter of an hour on any account, were glad to see him coming. The merchants in the little towns about the county missed him if he didn't drop in once a week or so. He was active in politics; never ran for an office himself, but often took up the cause of a friend and con-ducted his campaign for him.

The French saying, "Joy of the street, sorrow of the home," was exemplified in Mr. Wheeler, though not at all in the French way. His own affairs were of secondary importance to him. In the early days he had homesteaded and bought and leased enough land to make him rich. Now he had only to rent it out to good farmers who liked to work—he didn't, and of that he made no secret. When he was at home, he usually sat upstairs in the living room, reading newspapers. He subscribed for a dozen or more— the list included a weekly devoted to scandal—and he was well informed about what was going on in the world. He had magnificent health, and illness in himself or in other people struck him as humorous. To be sure, he never suffered from anything more perplexing than toothache or boils, or an occasional bilious attack.

Wheeler gave liberally to churches and charities, was always ready to lend money or machinery to a neighbour who was short of anything. He liked to tease and shock diffident people, and had an inexhaustible supply of funny stories. Everybody marvelled that he got on so well with his oldest son, Bayliss Wheeler. Not that Bayliss was exactly diffident, but he was a narrow-gauge fellow, the sort of prudent young man one wouldn't expect Nat Wheeler to like.

Bayliss had a farm implement business in Frankfort, and though he was still under thirty he had made a very considerable financial success. Perhaps Wheeler was proud of his son's business acumen. At any rate, he drove to town to see Bayliss several times a week, went to sales and stock exhibits with him, and sat about his store for hours at a stretch, joking with the farmers who came in. Wheeler had been a heavy drinker in his day, and was still a heavy feeder. Bayliss was thin and dyspeptic, and a virulent Prohibitionist; he would have liked to regulate everybody's diet by his own feeble constitution. Even Mrs. Wheeler, who took the men God had apportioned her for granted, wondered how Bayliss and his father could go off to conventions together and have a good time, since their ideas of what made a good time were so different.

Once every few years, Mr. Wheeler bought a new suit and a dozen stiff shirts and went back to Maine to visit his brothers and sisters, who were very quiet, conventional people. But he was always glad to get home to his old clothes, his big farm, his buckboard, and Bayliss.

Mrs. Wheeler had come out from Vermont to be Principal of the High School, when Frankfort was a frontier town and Nat Wheeler was a prosperous bachelor. He must have fancied her for the same reason he liked his son Bayliss,—because she was so different. There was this to be said for Nat Wheeler, that he liked every sort of human creature; he liked good people and honest people, and he liked rascals and hypocrites almost to the point of loving them. If he heard that a neighbour had played a sharp trick or done something particularly mean, he was sure to drive over to see the man at once, as if he hadn't hitherto appreciated him.

There was a large, loafing dignity about Claude's father. He liked to provoke others to uncouth laughter, but he never laughed immoderately himself. In telling stories about him, people often tried to imitate his smooth, senatorial voice, robust but never loud. Even when he was hilariously delighted by anything,—as when poor Mahailey, undressing in the dark on a summer night, sat down on the sticky fly-paper,—he was not boisterous. He was a jolly, easy-going father, indeed, for a boy who was not thin-skinned.

II

Claude and his mules rattled into Frankfort just as the calliope went screaming down Main Street at the head of the circus parade. Getting rid of his disagreeable freight and his uncongenial companions as soon as possible, he elbowed his way along the crowded sidewalk, looking for some of the neighbour boys. Mr. Wheeler was standing on the Farmer's Bank corner, towering a head above the throng, chaffing with a little hunchback who was setting up a shell-game. To avoid his father, Claude turned and went into his brother's store. The two big show windows were full of country children, their mothers standing behind them to watch the parade. Bayliss was seated in the little glass cage where he did his writing and bookkeeping. He nodded at Claude from his desk.

"Hello," said Claude, bustling in as if he were in a great hurry. "Have you seen Ernest Havel? I thought I might find him in here."

Bayliss swung round in his swivel chair to return a plough catalogue to the shelf. "What would he be in here for? Better look for him in the saloon." Nobody could put meaner insinuations into a slow, dry remark than Bayliss.

Claude's cheeks flamed with anger. As he turned away, he noticed something unusual about his brother's face, but he wasn't going to give him the satisfaction of asking him how he had got a black eye. Ernest Havel was a Bohemian, and he usually drank a glass of beer when he came to town; but he was sober and thoughtful beyond the wont of young men. From Bayliss' drawl one might have supposed that the boy was a drunken loafer.

At that very moment Claude saw his friend on the other side of the street, following the wagon of trained dogs that brought up the rear of the procession. He ran across, through a crowd of shouting youngsters, and caught Ernest by the arm.

"Hello, where are you off to?"

"I'm going to eat my lunch before show-time. I left my

wagon out by the pumping station, on the creek. What about you?"

"I've got no program. Can I go along?"

Ernest smiled. "I expect. I've got enough lunch for two."

"Yes, I know. You always have. I'll join you later."

Claude would have liked to take Ernest to the hotel for dinner. He had more than enough money in his pockets; and his father was a rich farmer. In the Wheeler family a new thrasher or a new automobile was ordered without a question, but it was considered extravagant to go to a hotel for dinner. If his father or Bayliss heard that he had been there—and Bayliss heard everything—they would say he was putting on airs, and would get back at him. He tried to excuse his cowardice to himself by saying that he was dirty and smelled of the hides; but in his heart he knew that he did not ask Ernest to go to the hotel with him because he had been so brought up that it would be difficult for him to do this simple thing. He made some purchases at the fruit stand and the cigar counter, and then hurried out along the dusty road toward the pumping station. Ernest's wagon was standing under the shade of some willow trees, on a little sandy bottom half enclosed by a loop of the creek which curved like a horseshoe. Claude threw himself on the sand beside the stream and wiped the dust from his hot face. He felt he had now closed the door on his disagreeable morning.

Ernest produced his lunch basket.

"I got a couple bottles of beer cooling in the creek," he said. "I knew you wouldn't want to go in a saloon."

"Oh, forget it!" Claude muttered, ripping the cover off

a jar of pickles. He was nineteen years old, and he was afraid to go into a saloon, and his friend knew he was afraid.

After lunch, Claude took out a handful of good cigars he had bought at the drugstore. Ernest, who couldn't afford cigars, was pleased. He lit one, and as he smoked he kept looking at it with an air of pride and turning it around between his fingers.

The horses stood with their heads over the wagon-box, munching their oats. The stream trickled by under the willow roots with a cool, persuasive sound. Claude and Ernest lay in the shade, their coats under their heads, talking very little. Occasionally a motor dashed along the road toward town, and a cloud of dust and a smell of gasoline blew in over the creek bottom; but for the most part the silence of the warm, lazy summer noon was undisturbed. Claude could usually forget his own vexations and chagrins when he was with Ernest. The Bohemian boy was never uncertain, was not pulled in two or three ways at once. He was simple and direct. He had a number of impersonal preoccupations; was interested in politics and history and in new inventions. Claude felt that his friend lived in an atmosphere of mental liberty to which he himself could never hope to attain. After he had talked with Ernest for awhile, the things that did not go right on the farm seemed less important.

Claude's mother was almost as fond of Ernest as he was himself. When the two boys were going to high school, Ernest often came over in the evening to study with Claude, and while they worked at the long kitchen table

Mrs. Wheeler brought her darning and sat near them, helping them with their Latin and algebra. Even old Mahailey was enlightened by their words of wisdom.

Mrs. Wheeler said she would never forget the night Ernest arrived from the Old Country. His brother, Joe Havel, had gone to Frankfort to meet him, and was to stop on the way home and leave some groceries for the Wheelers. The train from the east was late; it was ten o'clock that night when Mrs. Wheeler, waiting in the kitchen, heard Havel's wagon rumble across the little bridge over Lovely Creek. She opened the outside door, and presently Joe came in with a bucket of salt fish in one hand and a sack of flour on his shoulder. While he took the fish down to the cellar for her, another figure appeared in the doorway; a young boy, short, stooped, with a flat cap on his head and a great oilcloth valise, such as pedlars carry, strapped to his back. He had fallen asleep in the wagon, and on waking and finding his brother gone, had supposed they were at home and scrambled for his pack. He stood in the doorway, blinking his eyes at the light, looking astonished but eager to do whatever was required of him. What if one of her own boys, Mrs. Wheeler thought. . . . She went up to him and put her arm around him, laughing a little and saying in her quiet voice, just as if he could understand her, "Why, you're only a little boy after all, aren't you?"

Ernest said afterwards that it was his first welcome to this country, though he had travelled so far, and had been pushed and hauled and shouted at for so many days, he had lost count of them. That night he and Claude only shook hands and looked at each other suspiciously, but ever since they had been good friends.

After their picnic the two boys went to the circus in a happy frame of mind. In the animal tent they met big Leonard Dawson, the oldest son of one of the Wheelers' near neighbours, and the three sat together for the performance. Leonard said he had come to town alone in his car; wouldn't Claude ride out with him? Claude was glad enough to turn the mules over to Ralph, who didn't mind the hired men as much as he did.

Leonard was a strapping brown fellow of twenty-five, with big hands and feet, white teeth, and flashing eyes full of energy. He and his father and two brothers not only worked their own big farm, but rented a quarter section from Nat Wheeler. They were master farmers. If there was a dry summer and a failure, Leonard only laughed and stretched his long arms, and put in a bigger crop next year. Claude was always a little reserved with Leonard; he felt that the young man was rather contemptuous of the haphazard way in which things were done on the Wheeler place, and thought his going to college a waste of money. Leonard had not even gone through the Frankfort High School, and he was already a more successful man than Claude was ever likely to be. Leonard did think these things, but he was fond of Claude, all the same.

At sunset the car was speeding over a fine stretch of smooth road across the level country that lay between Frankfort and the rougher land along Lovely Creek. Leonard's attention was largely given up to admiring the faultless behaviour of his engine. Presently he chuckled to himself and turned to Claude.

"I wonder if you'd take it all right if I told you a joke on Bayliss?"

"I expect I would." Claude's tone was not at all eager.

"You saw Bayliss today? Notice anything queer about him, one eye a little off colour? Did he tell you how he got it?"

"No. I didn't ask him."

"Just as well. A lot of people did ask him, though, and he said he was hunting around his place for something in the dark and ran into a reaper. Well, I'm the reaper!"

Claude looked interested. "You mean to say Bayliss was in a fight?"

Leonard laughed. "Lord, no! Don't you know Bayliss? I went in there to pay a bill yesterday, and Susie Gray and another girl came in to sell tickets for the firemen's dinner. An advance man for this circus was hanging around, and he began talking a little smart,—nothing rough, but the way such fellows will. The girls handed it back to him, and sold him three tickets and shut him up. I couldn't see how Susie thought so quick what to say. The minute the girls went out Bayliss started knocking them; said all the country girls were getting too fresh and knew more than they ought to about managing sporty men—and right there I reached out and handed him one. I hit harder than I meant to. I meant to slap him, not to give him a black eye. But you can't always regulate things, and I was hot all over. I waited for him to come back at me. I'm bigger than he is, and I wanted to give him satisfaction. Well, sir, he never moved a muscle! He stood there getting redder and redder, and his eyes watered. I don't say he cried, but his eyes watered. 'All right, Bayliss,' said I. 'Slow with your fists, if that's your principle; but slow with your tongue, too,—especially when the parties mentioned aren't present.'"

"Bayliss will never get over that," was Claude's only comment.

"He don't have to!" Leonard threw up his head. "I'm a good customer; he can like it or lump it, till the price of binding twine goes down!"

For the next few minutes the driver was occupied with trying to get up a long, rough hill on high gear. Sometimes he could make that hill, and sometimes he couldn't, and he was not able to account for the difference. After he pulled the second lever with some disgust and let the car amble on as she would, he noticed that his companion was disconcerted.

"I'll tell you what, Leonard," Claude spoke in a strained voice. "I think the fair thing for you to do is to get out here by the road and give me a chance."

Leonard swung his steering wheel savagely to pass a wagon on the down side of the hill. "What the devil are you talking about, boy?"

"You think you've got our measure all right, but you ought to give me a chance first."

Leonard looked down in amazement at his own big brown hands, lying on the wheel. "You mortal fool kid, what would I be telling you all this for, if I didn't know you were another breed of cats? I never thought you got on too well with Bayliss yourself."

"I don't, but I won't have you thinking you can slap the men in my family whenever you feel like it." Claude knew that his explanation sounded foolish, and his voice, in spite of all he could do, was weak and angry.

Young Leonard Dawson saw he had hurt the boy's feelings. "Lord, Claude, I know you're a fighter. Bayliss never was. I went to school with him."

The ride ended amicably, but Claude wouldn't let Leonard take him home. He jumped out of the car with a curt good night, and ran across the dusky fields toward the light that shone from the house on the hill. At the little bridge over the creek, he stopped to get his breath and to be sure that he was outwardly composed before he went in to see his mother.

"Ran against a reaper in the dark!" he muttered aloud, clenching his fist.

Listening to the deep singing of the frogs, and to the distant barking of the dogs up at the house, he grew calmer. Nevertheless, he wondered why it was that one had sometimes to feel responsible for the behaviour of people whose natures were wholly antipathetic to one's own.

Chapter One

from THE PROFESSOR'S HOUSE

The moving was over and done. Professor St. Peter was alone in the dismantled house where he had lived ever since his marriage, where he had worked out his career and brought up his two daughters. It was almost as ugly as it is possible for a house to be; square, three stories in height, painted the colour of ashes—the front porch just too narrow for comfort, with a slanting floor and sagging steps. As he walked slowly about the empty, echoing rooms on that bright September morning, the Professor regarded thoughtfully the needless inconveniences he had put up with for so long; the stairs that were too steep, the halls that were too cramped, the awkward oak mantles with thick round posts crowned by bumptious wooden balls, over green-tiled fireplaces.

Certain wobbly stair treads, certain creaky boards in the upstairs hall, had made him wince many times a day for twenty-odd years—and they still creaked and wobbled. He had a deft hand with tools, he could easily have fixed them, but there were always so many things to fix, and there was not time enough to go round. He went into the kitchen, where he had carpentered under a succession of cooks, went up to the bath-room on the second floor, where there was only a painted tin tub; the taps were so old that no plumber could ever screw them tight enough to stop the drip, the window could only be coaxed up and down by wiggling, and the doors of the linen closet didn't fit. He had sympathized with his daughters' dissatisfaction, though he could never quite agree with them that the bath should be the most attractive room in the house. He had spent the happiest years of his youth in a house at Versailles where it distinctly was not, and he had known many charming people who had no bath at all. However, as his wife said: "If your country has contributed one thing, at least, to civilization, why not have it?" Many a night, after blowing out his study lamp, he had leaped into that tub, clad in his pyjamas, to give it another coat of some one of the many paints that were advertised to behave like porcelain, and didn't.

The Professor in pyjamas was not an unpleasant sight; for looks, the fewer clothes he had on, the better. Anything that clung to his body showed it to be built upon extremely good bones, with the slender hips and springy shoulders of a tireless swimmer. Though he was born on Lake Michigan, of mixed stock (Canadian French on one side, and American farmers on the other), St. Peter was commonly said to look like a Spaniard. That was possibly because he had been in Spain a good deal, and was an authority on certain phases of Spanish history. He had a long brown face, with an oval chin over which he wore a close-trimmed Van Dyke, like a tuft of shiny black fur. With this silky, very black hair, he had a tawny skin with gold lights in it, a hawk nose, and hawk-like eyes—brown and gold and green. They were set in ample cavities, with plenty of room to move about, under thick, curly, black eyebrows that turned up sharply at the outer ends, like military moustaches. His wicked-looking eyebrows made his students call him Mephistopheles—and there was no evading the searching eyes underneath them; eyes that in a flash could pick out a friend or an unusual stranger from a throng. They had lost none of their fire, though just now the man behind them was feeling a diminution of ardour.

His daughter Kathleen, who had done several successful studies of him in water-colour, had once said:—"The thing that really makes Papa handsome is the modelling of his head between the top of his ear and his crown; it is quite the best thing about him." That part of his head was high, polished, hard as bronze, and the close-growing black hair threw off a streak of light along the rounded ridge where the skull was fullest. The mould of his head on the side was so individual and definite, so far from casual, that it was more like a statue's head than a man's.

From one of the dismantled windows the Professor happened to look out into his back garden, and at that cheerful sight he went quickly downstairs and escaped from the dusty air and brutal light of the empty rooms.

His walled-in garden had been the comfort of his life—and it was the one thing his neighbours held against him. He started to make it soon after the birth of his first daughter, when his wife began to be unreasonable about his spending so much time at the lake and on the tennis court. In this undertaking he got help and encouragement from his landlord, a retired German farmer, good-natured and lenient about everything but spending money. If the Professor happened to have a new baby at home, or a faculty dinner, or an illness in the family, or any unusual expense, Appelhoff cheerfully waited for the rent; but pay for repairs he would not. When it was a question of the garden, however, the old man sometimes stretched a point. He helped his tenant with seeds and slips and sound advice, and with his twisted old back. He even spent a little money to bear half the expense of the stucco wall.

The Professor had succeeded in making a French garden in Hamilton. There was not a blade of grass; it was a tidy half-acre of glistening gravel and glistening shrubs and bright flowers. There were trees, of course; a spreading horse-chestnut, a row of slender Lombardy poplars at the back, along the white wall, and in the middle two symmetrical, round-topped linden-trees. Masses of green-brier grew in the corners, the prickly stems interwoven and clipped until they were like great bushes. There was a bed for salad herbs. Salmon-pink geraniums dripped over the wall. The French marigolds and dahlias were just now at their best—such dahlias as no one else in Hamilton could grow. St. Peter had tended this bit of ground for over twenty years, and had got the upper hand of it. In the spring, when homesickness for other lands and the fret of things unaccomplished awoke, he worked off his discontent here. In the long hot summers, when he could not go abroad, he stayed at home with his garden, sending his wife and daughters to Colorado to escape the humid prairie heat, so nourishing to wheat and corn, so exhausting to human beings. In those months when he was a bachelor again, he brought down his books and papers and worked in a deck chair under the linden-trees; breakfasted and lunched and had his tea in the garden. And it was there he and Tom Outland used to sit and talk half through the warm, soft nights.

On this September morning however, St. Peter knew that he could not evade the unpleasant effects of change by tarrying among his autumn flowers. He must plunge in like a man, and get used to the feeling that under his work-room there was a dead, empty house. He broke off a gera-nium blossom, and with it still in his hand went resolutely up two flights of stairs to the third floor where, under the slope of the mansard roof, there was one room still fur-nished—that is, if it had ever been furnished.

The low ceiling sloped down on three sides, the slant being interrupted on the east by a single square window, swinging outward on hinges and held ajar by a hook in the sill. This was the sole opening for light and air. Walls and ceiling alike were covered with a yellow paper which had once been very ugly, but had faded into inoffensive neu-trality. The matting on the floor was worn and scratchy. Against the wall stood an old walnut table, with one leaf up, holding piles of orderly papers. Before it was a cane-backed office chair that turned on a screw. This dark den had for many years been the Professor's study.

Downstairs, off the back parlour, he had a show study, with roomy shelves where his library was housed, and a proper desk at which he wrote letters. But it was a sham. This was the place where he worked. And not he alone. For three weeks in the fall, and again three in the spring, he shared his cuddy with Augusta, the sewing-woman, niece of his old landlord, a reliable, methodical spinster, a German Catholic and very devout.

Since Augusta finished her day's work at five o'clock, and the Professor, on week-days, worked here only at night, they did not elbow each other too much. Besides, neither was devoid of consideration. Every evening, before she left, Augusta swept up the scraps from the floor, rolled her patterns, closed the sewing-machine, and picked ravellings off the box-couch, so that there would be no threads to stick to the Professor's old smoking-jacket if he should happen to lie down for a moment in working-hours.

St. Peter, in his turn, when he put out his lamp after midnight, was careful to brush away ashes and tobacco crumbs—smoking was very distasteful to Augusta—and to open the hinged window back as far as it would go, on the second hook, so that the night wind might carry away the smell of his pipe as much as possible. The unfinished dresses which she left hanging on the forms, however, were often so saturated with smoke that he knew she found it a trial to work on them next morning.

These "forms" were the subject of much banter between them. The one which Augusta called "the bust" stood in the darkest corner of the room, upon a high wooden chest in which blankets and winter wraps were yearly stored. It was a headless, armless female torso, covered with strong black cotton, and so richly developed in the part for which it was named that the Professor once explained to Augusta how, in calling it so, she followed a natural law of language, termed, for convenience, metonymy. Augusta enjoyed the Professor when he was *risqué,* since she was sure of his ultimate delicacy. Though this figure looked so ample and billowy (as if you might lay your head upon its deep-breathing softness and rest safe forever), if you touched it you suffered a severe shock, no matter how many times you had touched it before. It presented the most unsympathetic surface imaginable. Its hardness was not that of wood, which responds to concussion with living vibration and is stimulating to the hand, nor that of felt, which drinks something from the fingers. It was a dead, opaque, lumpy solidity, like chunks of putty, or tightly packed sawdust—very disappointing to the tactile sense, yet somehow always fooling you again. For no matter how often you had bumped up against that torso, you could never believe that contact with it would be as bad as it was.

The second form was more self-revelatory; a full-length female figure in a smart wire skirt with a trim metal waist line. It had no legs, as one could see all too well, no viscera behind its glistening ribs, and its bosom resembled a strong wire bird-cage. But St. Peter contended that it had a nervous system. When Augusta left it clad for the night in a new party dress for Rosamond or Kathleen, it often took on a sprightly, tricky air, as if it were going out for the evening to make a great show of being harum-scarum, giddy, *folle*. It seemed just on the point of tripping downstairs, or on tiptoe, waiting for the waltz to begin. At times the wire lady was most convincing in her pose as a woman of light behaviour, but she never fooled St. Peter. He had his blind spots, but he had never been taken in by one of her kind!

Augusta had somehow got it into her head that these forms were unsuitable companions for one engaged in scholarly pursuits, and she periodically apologized for their presence when she came to install herself and fulfil her "time" at the house.

"Not at all, Augusta," the Professor had often said. "If they were good enough for *Monsieur Bergeret,* they are certainly good enough for me."

This morning, as St. Peter was sitting in his desk chair, looking musingly at the pile of papers before him, the door opened and there stood Augusta herself. How astonishing that he had not heard her heavy, deliberate tread on the now uncarpeted stair!

"Why, Professor St. Peter! I never thought of finding you here, or I'd have knocked. I guess we will have to do our moving together."

St. Peter had risen—Augusta loved his manners—but he offered her the sewing-machine chair and resumed his seat.

"Sit down, Augusta, and we'll talk it over. I'm not moving just yet—don't want to disturb all my papers. I'm staying on until I finish a piece of writing. I've seen your uncle about it. I'll work here, and board at the new house. But this is confidential. If it were noised about, people might begin to say that Mrs. St. Peter and I had—how do they put it, parted, separated?"

Augusta dropped her eyes in an indulgent smile. "I think people in your station would say separated."

"Exactly; a good scientific term, too. Well, we haven't, you know. But I'm going to write on here for a while."

"Very well, sir. And I won't always be getting in your way now. In the new house you have a beautiful study downstairs, and I have a light, airy room on the third floor."

"Where you won't smell smoke, eh?"

"Oh, Professor, I never really minded!" Augusta spoke with feeling. She rose and took up the black bust in her long arms.

The Professor also rose, very quickly. "What are you doing?"

She laughed. "Oh, I'm not going to carry them through the street, Professor! The grocery boy is downstairs with his cart, to wheel them over."

"Wheel them over?"

"Why, yes, to the new house, Professor. I've come a week before my regular time, to make curtains and hem linen for Mrs. St. Peter. I'll take everything over this morning except the sewing-machine—that's too heavy for the cart, so the boy will come back for it with the delivery wagon. Would you just open the door for me, please?"

"No, I won't! Not at all. You don't need her to make curtains. I can't have this room changed if I'm going to work here. He can take the sewing-machine—yes. But put her back on the chest where she belongs, please. She does very well there." St. Peter had got to the door, and stood with his back against it.

Augusta rested her burden on the edge of the chest.

"But next week I'll be working on Mrs. St. Peter's clothes, and I'll need the forms. As the boy's here, he'll just wheel them over," she said soothingly.

"I'm damned if he will! They shan't be wheeled. They stay right there in their own place. You shan't take away my ladies. I never heard of such a thing!"

Augusta was vexed with him now, and a little ashamed of him. "But, Professor, I can't work without my forms.

They've been in your way all these years, and you've always complained of them, so don't be contrary, sir."

"I never complained, Augusta. Perhaps of certain disappointments they recalled, or of cruel biological necessities they imply—but of them individually, never! Go and buy some new ones for your airy atelier, as many as you wish— I'm said to be rich now, am I not?—Go buy, but you can't have my women. That's final."

Augusta looked down her nose as she did at church when the dark sins were mentioned. "Professor," she said severely. "I think this time you are carrying a joke too far. You never used to." From the tilt of her chin he saw that she felt the presence of some improper suggestion.

"No matter what you think, you can't have them." They considered, both were in earnest now. Augusta was first to break the defiant silence.

"I suppose I am to be allowed to take my patterns?"

"Your patterns? Oh, yes, the cut-out things you keep in the couch with my old note-books? Certainly, you can have them. Let me lift it for you." He raised the hinged top of the box-couch that stood against the wall, under the slope of the ceiling. At one end of the upholstered box were piles of note-books and bundles of manuscript tied up in square packages with mason's cord. At the other end were many little rolls of patterns, cut out of newspapers and tied with bits of ribbon, gingham, silk, georgette; notched charts which followed the changing stature and figures of the Misses St. Peter from early childhood to womanhood. In the middle of the box, patterns and manuscripts interpenetrated.

"I see we shall have some difficulty in separating our

life work, Augusta. We've kept our papers together a long while now."

"Yes, Professor. When I first came to sew for Mrs. St. Peter, I never thought I should grow grey in her service."

He started. What other future could Augusta possibly have expected? This disclosure amazed him.

"Well, well, we mustn't think mournfully of it, Augusta. Life doesn't turn out for any of us as we plan." He stood and watched her large slow hands travel about among the little packets, as she put them into his waste-basket to carry them down to the cart. He had often wondered how she managed to sew with hands that folded and unfolded as rigidly as umbrellas—no light French touch about Augusta; when she sewed on a bow, it stayed there. She herself was tall, large-boned, flat and stiff, with a plain, solid face, and brown eyes not destitute of fun. As she knelt by the couch, sorting her patterns, he stood beside her, his hand on the lid, though it would have stayed up unsupported. Her last remark had troubled him.

"What a fine lot of hair you have, Augusta! You know I think it's rather nice, that grey wave on each side. Gives it character. You'll never need any of this false hair that's in all the shop windows."

"There's altogether too much of that, Professor. So many of my customers are using it now—ladies you wouldn't expect would. They say most of it was cut off the heads of dead Chinamen. Really, it's got to be such a frequent thing that the priest spoke against it only last Sunday."

"Did he, indeed? Why, what could he say? Seems such a personal matter."

"Well, he said it was getting to be a scandal in the Church, and a priest couldn't go to see a pious woman any more without finding switches and rats and transformations lying about her room, and it was disgusting."

"Goodness gracious, Augusta! What business has a priest going to see a woman in the room where she takes off these ornaments—or to see her without them?"

Augusta grew red, and tried to look angry, but her laugh narrowly missed being a giggle. "He goes to give them the Sacrament, of course, Professor! You've made up your mind to be contrary to-day, haven't you?"

"You relieve me greatly. Yes, I suppose in cases of sudden illness the hair would be lying about where it was lightly taken off. But as you first quoted the priest, Augusta, it was rather shocking. You'll never convert me back to the religion of my fathers now, if you're going to sew in the new house and I'm going to work on here. Who is ever to remind me when it's All Souls' Day or Ember Day, or Maundy Thursday, or anything?"

Augusta said she must be leaving. St. Peter heard her well-known tread as she descended the stairs. How much she reminded him of, to be sure! She had been most at the house in the days when his daughters were little girls and needed so many clean frocks. It was in those very years that he was beginning his great work; when the desire to do it and the difficulties attending such a project strove together in his mind like Macbeth's two spent swimmers—years when he had the courage to say to himself: "I will do this dazzling, this beautiful, this utterly impossible thing!"

During the fifteen years he had been working on his *Spanish Adventurers in North America,* this room had been his centre of operations. There had been delightful excursions and digressions; the two Sabbatical years when he was in Spain studying records, two summers in the Southwest on the trail of his adventurers, another in Old Mexico, dashes to France to see his foster-brothers. But the notes and the records and the ideas always came back to this room. It was here they were digested and sorted, and woven into their proper place in his history.

Fairly considered, the sewing-room was the most inconvenient study a man could possibly have, but it was the one place in the house where he could get isolation, insulation from the engaging drama of domestic life. No one was tramping over him, and only a vague sense, generally pleasant, of what went on below came up the narrow stairway. There were certainly no other advantages. The furnace heat did not reach the third floor. There was no way to warm the sewing-room, except by a rusty, round gas stove with no flue—a stove which consumed gas imperfectly and contaminated the air. To remedy this, the window must be left open—otherwise, with the ceiling so low, the air would speedily become unfit to breathe. If the stove were turned down, and the window left open a little way, a sudden gust of wind would blow the wretched thing out altogether, and a deeply absorbed man might be asphyxiated before he knew it. The Professor had found that the best method, in winter, was to turn the gas on full and keep the window wide on the hook, even if he had to put on a leather jacket over his working-coat. By that arrangement he had somehow managed to get air enough to work by.

He wondered now why he had never looked about for a better stove, a newer model; or why he had not at least painted this one, flaky with rust. But he had been able to get on only by neglecting negative comforts. He was by no means an ascetic. He knew that he was terribly selfish about personal pleasures, fought for them. If a thing gave him delight, he got it, if he sold his shirt for it. By doing without many so-called necessities he had managed to have his luxuries. He might, for instance, have had a convenient electric drop-light attached to the socket above his writing-table. Preferably, he wrote by a faithful kerosene lamp which he filled and tended himself. But sometimes he found that the oil-can in the closet was empty; then, to get more, he would have had to go down through the house to the cellar, and on his way he would almost surely become interested in what the children were doing, or in what his wife was doing—or he would notice that the kitchen linoleum was breaking under the sink where the maid kicked it up, and he would stop to tack it down. On that perilous journey down through the human house he might lose his mood, his enthusiasm, even his temper. So when the lamp was empty—and that usually occurred when he was in the middle of a most important passage—he jammed an eyeshade on his forehead and worked by the glare of that tormenting pear-shaped bulb, sticking out of the wall on a short curved neck just about four feet above his table. It was hard on eyes even as good as his. But once at his desk, he didn't dare quit it. He had found that you can train the mind to be active at a fixed time, just as the stomach is trained to be hungry at certain hours of the day.

If someone in the family happened to be sick, he didn't go to his study at all. Two evenings of the week he spent with his wife and daughters, and one evening he and his wife went out to dinner, or to the theatre or a concert.

That left him only four. He had Saturdays and Sundays, of course, and on those two days he worked like a miner under a landslide. Augusta was not allowed to come on Saturday, though she was paid for that day. All the while that he was working so fiercely by night, he was earning his living during the day; carrying full university work and feeding himself out to hundreds of students in lectures and consultations. But that was another life.

St. Peter had managed for years to live two lives, both of them very intense. He would willingly have cut down on his university work, would willingly have given his students chaff and sawdust—many instructors had nothing else to give them and got on very well—but his misfortune was that he loved youth—he was weak to it, it kindled him. If there was one eager eye, one doubting, critical mind, one lively curiosity in a whole lecture-room full of commonplace boys and girls, he was its servant. That ardour could command him. It hadn't worn out with years, this responsiveness, any more than the magnetic currents wear out; it had nothing to do with Time.

But he had burned his candle at both ends to some purpose—he had got what he wanted. By many petty economies of purse, he had managed to be extravagant with not a cent in the world but his professor's salary—he didn't, of course, touch his wife's small income from her father. By eliminations and combinations so many and subtle that it now made his head ache to think of them, he had done full justice to his university lectures, and at the same time carried on an engrossing piece of creative work. A man can do anything if he wishes to enough, St. Peter believed. Desire is creation, is the magical element in that process. If there were an instrument by which to measure desire, one could foretell achievement. He had been able to measure it, roughly, just once, in his student Tom Outland,—and he had foretold.

There was one fine thing about this room that had been the scene of so many defeats and triumphs. From the window he could see, far away, just on the horizon, a long, blue, hazy smear—Lake Michigan, the inland sea of his childhood. Whenever he was tired and dull, when the white pages before him remained blank or were full of scratched-out sentences, then he left his desk, took the train to a little station twelve miles away, and spent a day on the lake with his sail-boat; jumping out to swim, floating on his back alongside, then climbing into his boat again.

When he remembered his childhood, he remembered blue water. There were certain human figures against it, of course; his practical, strong-willed Methodist mother, his gentle, weaned-away Catholic father, the old Kanuck grandfather, various brothers and sisters. But the great fact in life, the always possible escape from dullness, was the lake. The sun rose out of it, the day began there; it was like an open door that nobody could shut. The land and all its dreariness could never close in on you. You had only to look at the lake, and you knew you would soon be free. It was the first thing one saw in the morning, across the rugged cow pasture studded with shaggy pines, and it ran through the days like the weather, not a thing thought about, but a part of consciousness itself. When the ice chunks came in of a winter morning, crumbly and white, throwing off gold and rose-coloured reflections from a copper-coloured sun behind the grey clouds, he didn't observe the detail or

know what it was that made him happy; but now, forty
years later, he could recall all its aspects perfectly. They had
made pictures in him when he was unwilling and unconscious, when his eyes were merely open wide.

When he was eight years old, his parents sold the lake-
side farm and dragged him and his brothers and sisters out
to the wheat lands of central Kansas. St. Peter nearly died
of it. Never could he forget the few moments on the train
when that sudden, innocent blue across the sand dunes was
dying forever from his sight. It was like sinking for the third
time. No later anguish, and he had had his share, went so
deep or seemed so final. Even in his long, happy student
years with the Thierault family in France, that stretch of
blue water was the one thing he was home-sick for. In the
summer he used to go with the Thierault boys to Brittany
or to the Languedoc coast; but his lake was itself, as the
Channel and the Mediterranean were themselves. "No,"
he used to tell the boys, who were always asking him about
le Michigan, "it is altogether different. It is a sea, and yet is
not salt. It is blue, but quite another blue. Yes, there are
clouds and mists and sea-gulls, but—I don't know, *il est tou-
jours plus naïf.*"

Afterward, when St. Peter was looking for a professor-
ship, because he was very much in love and must marry at
once, out of the several positions offered him he took the
one at Hamilton, not because it was the best, but because
it seemed to him that any place near the lake was a place
where one could live. The sight of it from his study window these many years had been of more assistance than all
the convenient things he had done without would have
been.

Just in that corner, under Augusta's archaic "forms," he had always meant to put the filing-cabinets he had never spared the time or money to buy. They would have held all his notes and pamphlets, and the spasmodic rough drafts of passages far ahead. But he had never got them, and now he really didn't need them; it would be like locking the stable after the horse is stolen. For the horse was gone—that was the thing he was feeling most just now. In spite of all he'd neglected, he had completed his *Spanish Adventurers* in eight volumes—without filing-cabinets or money or a decent study or a decent stove—and without encouragement, Heaven knew! For all the interest the first three volumes awoke in the world, he might as well have dropped them into Lake Michigan. They had been timidly reviewed by other professors of history, in technical and educational journals. Nobody saw that he was trying to do something quite different—they merely thought he was trying to do the usual thing, and had not succeeded very well. They recommended to him the more even and genial style of John Fiske.

St. Peter hadn't, he could honestly say, cared a whoop—not in those golden days. When the whole plan of his narrative was coming clearer and clearer all the time, when he could feel his hand growing easier with his material, when all the foolish conventions about that kind of writing were falling away and his relation with his work was becoming every day more simple, natural, and happy,—he cared as little as the Spanish Adventurers themselves what Professor So-and-So thought about them. With the fourth volume he began to be aware that a few young men, scattered about the United States and England, were intensely interested in his experiment. With the fifth and sixth, they began to express their interest in lectures and in print. The two last volumes brought him a certain international reputation and what were called rewards—among them, the Oxford prize for history, with its five thousand pounds, which had built him the new house into which he did not want to move.

"Godfrey," his wife had gravely said one day, when she detected an ironical turn in some remark he made about the new house, "is there something you would rather have done with that money than to have built a house with it?"

"Nothing, my dear, nothing. If with that cheque I could have bought back the fun I had writing my history, you'd never have got your house. But one couldn't get that for twenty thousand dollars. The great pleasures don't come so cheap. There is nothing else, thank you."

December Night

from DEATH COMES FOR
THE ARCHBISHOP

Father Vaillant had been absent in Arizona since mid-summer, and it was now December. Bishop Latour had been going through one of those periods of coldness and doubt which, from his boyhood, had occasionally settled down upon his spirit and made him feel an alien, wherever he was. He attended to his correspondence, went on his rounds among the parish priests, held services at missions that were without pastors, superintended the building of the addition to the Sisters' school; but his heart was not in these things.

One night about three weeks before Christmas he was lying in his bed, unable to sleep, with the sense of failure clutching at his heart. His prayers were empty words and brought him no refreshment. His soul had become a barren field. He had nothing within himself to give his priests or his people. His work seemed superficial, a house built upon the sands. His great diocese was still a heathen country. The Indians travelled their old road of fear and darkness, battling with evil omens and ancient shadows. The Mexicans were children who played with their religion.

As the night wore on, the bed on which the Bishop lay became a bed of thorns; he could bear it no longer. Getting up in the dark, he looked out of the window and was surprised to find that it was snowing, that the ground was already lightly covered. The full moon, hidden by veils of cloud, threw a pale phosphorescent luminousness over the heavens, and the towers of the church stood up black against the silvery fleece. Father Latour felt a longing to go into the church to pray; but instead he lay down again under his blankets. Then, realizing that it was the cold of the church he shrank from, and despising himself, he rose again, dressed quickly, and went out into the court, throwing on over his cassock that faithful old cloak that was the twin of Father Vaillant's.

They had bought the cloth for those coats in Paris, long ago, when they were young men staying at the Seminary for Foreign Missions in the rue du Bac, preparing for their first voyage to the New World. The cloth had been made up into caped riding-cloaks by a German tailor in Ohio, and lined with fox fur. Years afterward, when Father Latour was about to start on his long journey in search of his Bishopric, that same tailor had made the cloaks over and relined them with squirrel skins, as more appropriate for a mild climate. These memories and many others went through the Bishop's mind as he wrapped the trusty garment about him and crossed the court to the sacristy, with the big iron key in his hand.

The court was white with snow, and the shadows of

walls and buildings stood out sharply in the faint light from the moon muffled in vapour. In the deep doorway of the sacristy he saw a crouching figure—a woman, he made out, and she was weeping bitterly. He raised her up and took her inside. As soon as he had lit a candle, he recognized her, and could have guessed her errand.

It was an old Mexican woman, called Sada, who was slave in an American family. They were Protestants, very hostile to the Roman Church, and they did not allow her to go to Mass or to receive the visits of a priest. She was carefully watched at home,—but in winter, when the heated rooms of the house were desirable to the family, she was put to sleep in a woodshed. Tonight, unable to sleep for the cold, she had gathered courage for this heroic action, had slipped out through the stable door and come running up an alley-way to the House of God to pray. Finding the front doors of the church fastened, she had made her way into the Bishop's garden and come round to the sacristy, only to find that, too, shut against her.

The Bishop stood holding the candle and watching her face while she spoke her few words; a dark brown peon face, worn thin and sharp by life and sorrow. It seemed to him that he had never seen pure goodness shine out of a human countenance as it did from hers. He saw that she had no stockings under her shoes,—the cast-off rawhides of her master,—and beneath her frayed black shawl was only a thin calico dress, covered with patches. Her teeth struck together as she stood trying to control her shivering. With one movement of his free hand the Bishop took the furred cloak from his shoulders and put it about her. This frightened her. She cowered under it, murmuring, "Ah, no, no, Padre!"

"You must obey your Padre, my daughter. Draw that cloak about you, and we will go into the church to pray."

The church was utterly black except for the red spark of the sanctuary lamp before the high altar. Taking her hand, and holding the candle before him, he led her across the choir to the Lady Chapel. There he began to light the tapers before the Virgin. Old Sada fell on her knees and kissed the floor. She kissed the feet of the Holy Mother, the pedestal on which they stood, crying all the while. But from the working of her face, from the beautiful tremors which passed over it, he knew they were tears of ecstasy.

"Nineteen years, Father; nineteen years since I have seen the holy things of the altar!"

"All that is passed, Sada. You have remembered the holy things in your heart. We will pray together."

The Bishop knelt beside her, and they began, *O Holy Mary, Queen of Virgins. . . .*

More than once Father Vaillant had spoken to the Bishop of this aged captive. There had been much whispering among the devout women of the parish about her pitiful case. The Smiths, with whom she lived, were Georgia people, who had at one time lived in El Paso del Norte, and they had taken her back to their native State with them. Not long ago some disgrace had come upon this family in Georgia; they had been forced to sell all their Negro slaves and flee the State. The Mexican woman they could not sell because they had no legal title to her; her position was irregular. Now that they were back in a Mex-

ican country, the Smiths were afraid their charwoman
might escape from them and find asylum among her own
people, so they kept strict watch upon her. They did not
allow her to go outside their own *patio,* not even to accompany her mistress to market.

Two women of the Altar Guild had been so bold as to
go into the *patio* to talk with Sada when she was washing
clothes, but they had been rudely driven away by the mistress of the house. Mrs. Smith had come running out into
the court, half dressed, and told them that if they had business at her *casa* they were to come in by the front door, and
not sneak in through the stable to frighten a poor silly creature. When they said they had come to ask Sada to go to
Mass with them, she told them she had got the poor creature out of the clutches of the priests once, and would see
to it that she did not fall into them again.

Even after that rebuff a very pious neighbour woman
had tried to say a word to Sada through the alley door of
the stable, where she was unloading wood off the burro.
But the old servant had put her finger to her lips and
motioned the visitor away, glancing back over her shoulder
the while with such an expression of terror that the intruder
hastened off, surmising that Sada would be harshly used if
she were caught speaking to anyone. The good woman
went immediately to Father Vaillant with this story, and he
had consulted the Bishop, declaring that something ought
to be done to secure the consolations of religion for the
bond-woman. But the Bishop replied that the time was not
yet; for the present it was inexpedient to antagonize these
people. The Smiths were the leaders of a small group of
low-caste Protestants who took every occasion to make

trouble for the Catholics. They hung about the door of the church on festival days with mockery and loud laughter, spoke insolently to the nuns in the street, stood jeering and blaspheming when the procession went by on Corpus Christi Sunday. There were five sons in the Smith family, fellows of low habits and evil tongues. Even the two younger boys, still children, showed a vicious disposition. Tranquilino had repeatedly driven these two boys out of the Bishop's garden, where they came with their lewd companions to rob the young pear trees or to speak filth against the priests.

When they rose from their knees, Father Latour told Sada he was glad to know that she remembered her prayers so well.

"Ah, Padre, every night I say my Rosary to my Holy Mother, no matter where I sleep!" declared the old creature passionately, looking up into his face and pressing her knotted hands against her breast.

When he asked if she had her beads with her, she was confused. She kept them tied with a cord around her waist, under her clothes, as the only place she could hide them safely.

He spoke soothingly to her. "Remember this, Sada; in the year to come, and during the Novena before Christmas, I will not forget to pray for you whenever I offer the Blessed Sacrifice of the Mass. Be at rest in your heart, for I will remember you in my silent supplications before the altar as I do my own sisters and my nieces."

Never, as he afterward told Father Vaillant, had it been permitted him to behold such deep experience of the holy joy of religion as on that pale December night. He was able to feel, kneeling beside her, the preciousness of the things of the altar to her who was without possessions; the tapers, the image of the Virgin, the figures of the saints, the Cross that took away indignity from suffering and made pain and poverty a means of fellowship with Christ. Kneeling beside the much enduring bond-woman, he experienced those holy mysteries as he had done in his young manhood. He seemed able to feel all it meant to her to know that there was a Kind Woman in Heaven, though there were such cruel ones on earth. Old people, who have felt blows and toil and known the world's hard hand, need, even more than children do, a woman's tenderness. Only a Woman, divine, could know all that a woman can suffer.

Not often, indeed, had Jean Marie Latour come so near to the Fountain of all Pity as in the Lady Chapel that night; the pity that no man born of woman could ever utterly cut himself off from; that was for the murderer on the scaffold, as it was for the dying solider or the martyr on the rack. The beautiful concept of Mary pierced the priest's heart like a sword.

"O Sacred Heart of Mary!" she murmured by his side, and he felt how that name was food and raiment, friend and mother to her. He received the miracle in her heart into his own, saw through her eyes, knew that his poverty was as bleak as hers. When the Kingdom of Heaven had first come into the world, into a cruel world of torture and slaves and masters, He who brought it had said, *"And whosoever is least among you, the same shall be first in the Kingdom of Heaven."* This church was Sada's house, and he was a servant in it.

The Bishop heard the old woman's confession. He blessed her and put both hands upon her head. When he took her down the nave to let her out of the church, Sada made to lift his cloak from her shoulders. He restrained her, telling her she must keep it for her own, and sleep in it at night. But she slipped out of it hurriedly; such a thought seemed to terrify her. "No, no, Father. If they were to find it on me!" More than that, she did not accuse her oppressors. But as she put it off, she stroked the old garment and patted it as if it were a living thing that had been kind to her.

Happily Father Latour bethought him of a little silver medal, with a figure of the Virgin, he had in his pocket. He gave it to her, telling her that it had been blessed by the Holy Father himself. Now she would have a treasure to hide and guard, to adore while her watchers slept. Ah, he thought, for one who cannot read—or think—the Image, the physical form of Love!

He fitted the great key into its lock, the door swung slowly back on its wooden hinges. The peace without seemed all one with the peace in his own soul. The snow had stopped, the gauzy clouds that had ribbed the arch of heaven were now all sunk into one soft white fog bank over the Sangre de Cristo mountains. The full moon shone high in the blue vault, majestic, lonely, benign. The Bishop stood in the doorway of his church, lost in thought, looking at the line of black footprints his departing visitor had left in the wet scurf of snow.

Collected Stories

In these nineteen stories you will find the great themes that Cather staked out like tracts of land: the plight of people hungry for beauty in a country that has no room for it; the mysterious arc of human lives; and the ways in which the American frontier transformed the strangers who came to it, turning them imperceptibly into Americans.
Fiction/Literature/0-679-73648-4

Death Comes for the Archbishop

This is the story of a single human life, lived simply in the silence of the desert. In 1851 Father Jean Marie Latour brings his faith to New Mexico—American by law but Mexican and Indian in custom and belief—and must endure the unforgiving landscape and his own loneliness.
Fiction/Literature/0-679-72889-9

A Lost Lady

To the people of Sweet Water, a fading railroad town on the Western plains, Mrs. Forrester is the resident aristocrat, at once gracious and comfortably remote. To her aging husband she is a treasure whose value increases as his powers fail. In this masterpiece of nuance and revelation, Willa Cather composed an answer to *Madame Bovary.*
Fiction/Literature/0-679-72887-2

Lucy Gayheart

At the age of eighteen, Lucy Gayheart heads for Chicago to study music. She is beautiful and impressionable and ardent, and these qualities attract the attention of Clement Sebastian, an aging but charismatic singer who exercises all the tragic, sinister fascination of a man who has renounced life only to turn back to seize it one last time.

Fiction/Literature/0-679-72888-0

My Ántonia

In this symphonically powerful novel, Willa Cather created one of the most winning heroines in American fiction, a woman whose robust high spirits and calm, undemonstrative strength make her emblematic of the virtues Cather most admired in her country.

Fiction/Literature/0-679-74187-9

My Mortal Enemy

Willa Cather's protagonist in *My Mortal Enemy* is Myra Henshawe, who as a young woman gave up a fortune to marry for love—a boldly romantic gesture that became a legend in her family. But this worldly, sarcastic, and perhaps even wicked woman may have been made for something greater than love. *My Mortal Enemy* is a work whose drama and intensely moral imagination make it unforgettable.

Fiction/Literature/0-679-73179-2

O Pioneers!

Cather's heroine is Alexandra Bergson, who arrives on the windblasted prairie of Hanover, Nebraska, as a girl and grows up to make it a prosperous farm. No other work of fiction so faithfully conveys both the sharp physical realities and the mythic sweep of the transformation of the American frontier.

Fiction/Literature/0-679-74362-6

One of Ours

Claude Wheeler, the sensitive, aspiring protagonist of this beautifully modulated novel, is the youngest son of a peculiarly American fairy tale. His fortune is ready-made for him, but he refuses to settle for it. Alienated from his crass father and pious mother, all but rejected by a wife who reserves her ardor for missionary work, Claude is an idealist without an ideal to cling to. It is only when he enters the First World War that Claude finds what he has been searching for all his life. Winner of the Pulitzer Prize.

Fiction/Literature/0-679-73744-8

The Professor's House

Professor Godfrey St. Peter is a man in his fifties who has devoted his life to his work, his wife, his garden, and his daughters. But when St. Peter is called on to move to a new house, a resistance develops which comes to encompass the entire order of his life.

Fiction/Literature/0-679-73180-6

Sapphira and the Slave Girl

One of Willa Cather's later works, this story of Sapphira Dodderige, a Virginia lady of the nineteenth century who marries beneath her and becomes irrationally jealous of Nancy, a beautiful slave, is considered by many one of her best novels.

Fiction/Literature/0-394-71434-2

Shadows on the Rock

In 1697, Quebec is an island of French civilization perched on a bare rock amid a wilderness of trackless forests. But to twelve-year-old Cécile Auclair, the rock is home. As Cather follows this devout and resourceful child over the course of a year, she re-creates the continent as it must have appeared to its first European inhabitants.

Fiction/Literature/0-679-76404-6

The Song of the Lark

Thea Kronborg, a minister's daughter in a provincial Colorado town, seems destined from childhood for a place in the wider world. But as her path to the world stage leads her ever farther from the humble town she can't forget and from the man she can't afford to love, Thea learns that her exceptional musical talent and fierce ambition are not enough. *The Song of the Lark* is a powerful portrait of the self-making of an artist.

Fiction/Literature/0-375-70645-3

VINTAGE **READERS**

Authors available in this series

Martin Amis

Nicholson Baker

James Baldwin

A. S. Byatt

Willa Cather

Sandra Cisneros

Joan Didion

Richard Ford

Langston Hughes

Barry Lopez

Alice Munro

Haruki Murakami

Vladimir Nabokov

V. S. Naipaul

Michael Ondaatje

Oliver Sacks

Representing a wide spectrum of some of our most significant modern authors, the Vintage Readers offer an attractive, accessible selection of writing that matters.